MW01277735

So . . . I lied. I wasn't used to lying and didn't like doing it but I had a good reason— truly I did.

— FOSTER LUTZ

Winner of the 20th Annual
International Three-Day
Novel-Writing Contest . . .

The Underwood

P.G. TARR

ANVIL PRESS PUBLISHERS

THE UNDERWOOD
Copyright © 1998 by P.G. Tarr

All rights reserved. No part of this book may be reproduced by any means without the prior written permission of the publisher, with the exception of brief passages in reviews. Any request for photocopying or other reprographic copying of any part of this book must be directed in writing to the Canadian Reprography Collective (CANCOPY), 6 Adelaide Street East, Suite 900, Toronto, Ontario, Canada, M5C 1H6.

CANADIAN CATALOGUING IN PUBLICATION DATA

Tarr, P.G. (Patrick G.) 1970-
The Underwood

ISBN 1-895636-17-5
I. Title
PS8589.A8686U52 1998   C813'.54   C98-910393-5
PR9199.3.T345U52 1998

PUBLISHED BY
Anvil Press
Suite 204-A – 175 East Broadway,
Vancouver, BC V5T 1W2 CANADA

FIRST EDITION
COVER DESIGN: B. Kaufman
COVER PHOTO: Edward Morrison

The publisher gratefully acknowledges the assistance of the B.C. Arts Council and the Canada Council for the Arts.

LE CONSEIL DES ARTS | THE CANADA COUNCIL
DU CANADA | FOR THE ARTS
DEPUIS 1957 | SINCE 1957

Represented in Canada by the Literary Press Group
Distributed by General Distribution Services.

PRINTED AND BOUND IN CANADA

Thanks To:

My family, Brian Kaufman & Anvil Press/sub-TERRAIN,
Cassandra Cronenberg, Matt Petrillo, Larissa Petrillo,
Duncan Blair, Nancy Friedland, Brett Burlock, Zak Cross,
Trudy Alexander, Sarah Iwakabe, Brent Summers,
Nancy McIlvaney, James MacDonald, Keith Toms,
Zwerina Golbohantosanquist, Tristen Bakker
and Matt Lumley.

DEC 2 9 1998

CHAPTER ONE

So . . . I LIED. I WASN'T USED TO LYING AND DIDN'T like doing it but I had a good reason—truly I did. I bet some people get so they don't even have to think about it, so it comes like sleeping or chewing or walking up stairs, but it never did for me. I just lied that one time.

Then he said, "How about it son, do you have what it takes to live up to our standards of excellence in entertainment?"

"Yes, I think I do."

"You think?"

"No. I mean yes. Definitely I do."

Mr. Breedle leaned back in his chair, gave me a rigid smile, and plucked another mint from the blue glass ashtray on the desk. He bit into it and it made a sound like the crack of a starter's pistol. I felt like sprinting. He sighed and he crunched and then he reached for another mint. Sometimes I count things—

sometimes when I'm jittery. That was his seventh mint in five minutes.

"I don't know," he said. "How old did you say you were?"

"I'm twenty-nine. This summer."

"Hmmm. You see, usually our performers are more . . . seasoned."

"But you liked my audition?"

He pretended to think about it. I knew that he had because I was watching his face while I played. We sat like this for a few seconds while the heating system began to growl and pound. Finally he said, "Yes, Foster, I liked it very much. It reminded me of the music of The Underwood's glory days. Simple and lovely. Very lovely indeed."

With this I lost him to reverie. His grey moustache began to twitch, out of place beneath a unified clump of jet black hair. It looked as if it wanted to be somewhere else. We were comrades, his moustache and I— I wanted to be down in the lounge, back at the piano.

Mr. Breedle wore a black pinstriped suit and a black bow tie. There were silver cufflinks on his wrists and the silver chain of a pocket watch gleamed its way across the fabric of his jacket. I think he fancied himself an artifact of those glory days he'd mentioned four times already. The man was a walking museum, always open.

In comparison, his office was plain. There was little to speak of other than the chairs we sat on, the desk that separated us, and a single withering fern behind him by the window, although there was room for much more. The paint was smoke-steeped and poised to shudder off the walls in large, limp sheets. There was a basement smell despite the fact that we were on the second floor. Up here in Management the glory days were over.

"Mr. Breedle?" I said, and he hobbled back to the present. "So what about the job? Am I hired?"

He clasped his hands together and looked me square in the forehead. I guess he found an answer there because in a voice waxy with portent he said, "Yes, young man, you get the job. Knock 'em dead, as they say." If we'd been closer he might have clapped me on the shoulder. I was glad we weren't closer.

He paused then, serious, pained by matters of finance.

"Here are the details of your employment: you'll be paid two hundred dollars a week and provided with a room in the hotel. See Manny at the front desk about a key. You pay for meals in the hotel restaurant but there is an employee discount of twenty percent. I'd like you to start tonight. Are you prepared?"

With this his eyebrows arched nearly to his hairline. It was stunning.

"Yes sir, I am."

We shook hands then and I thanked him. He didn't see me to the door but ate another mint and said as he chewed it, "You are now part of an important legacy. I expect you to treat that legacy with the greatest of respect."

"I will, Mr. Breedle, I promise."

I stepped into the cold fluorescence of the waiting room and closed the door behind me. It was a tiny, heartless space. The receptionist sat at a cluttered expanse of desk holding a pencil over a blank sheet of paper. Behind her there was a calendar two years out of date. Everything about her yearned to blend into the deep wood paneling on the walls. She was almost there.

"Sooo?"

"So I guess I work here."

She took off her glasses. "That's nice. The man before you—Lloyd—he left." She looked at the telephone in front of her as if it might tell her what to say next. When it didn't she said, "Hmmmm."

"Can I ask you something?"

This startled her. I doubted that people asked her things very often. "Oh. Of course you can dear."

"The mints?"

A smile flitted across her face but never really took hold. "Mr. Breedle used to smoke quite a bit, you see.

The mints are by way of a substitute."

"What happens when he runs out?"

She pitched a glance at the office door and then beckoned me closer. She whispered, "Oh dear. I make sure he never runs out. But if he did . . . if he did I imagine he'd come crawling out here to eat *me*."

She began to laugh but it caught in her throat and turned into a cough. It was an odd-sounding cough because she actually said the word as she did it: "*Cough, cough, cough*."

I excused myself, wary of the wall woman, and turned to the door. "I guess I'll be seeing you."

"Yes dear. *Cough*. Have a nice day. Settle in."

The phone rang as I put my hand on the door-knob and I heard her clear her throat. "This is The Underwood," she said.

I went out into the hallway. It was teeming with pictures. I hadn't paid them much attention on my way in; I was too nervous then. But with the interview out of the way I decided to take my time so I could look at every single one.

Most of the pictures were in black and white; as the years went by the photography became worse and the frames cheapened from carved wood to dull brown plastic. There were hardly any shots from recent years.

The first pictures were of the construction of the hotel in the late 40s. All the workers looked like veterans, happy that they were building a hotel instead of shooting at people. They smiled as they lay the foundation and they smiled as they strutted across thick steel beams four storeys in the air.

There was a picture of a man in a tuxedo smashing a bottle of champagne against the hotel's façade. He was surrounded by people who seemed shocked that he was smashing the bottle instead of opening it—even he seemed shocked.

After that came a cluster of pictures from the 50s. When I saw them I understood Mr. Breedle's nostalgia. There were pictures of movie stars, singers, mobsters, and a whole lot of other people who I didn't recognize but who had a kind of size about them: it was as if they resented being cooped up inside their frames. "Let me out," they said.

Halfway down the hall I came across a picture that I couldn't believe. The picture was signed and affixed with a caption: 'The Underwood Hotel, 1950.' It was Nat King Cole, sitting at a piano in the same lounge where I'd played my audition. With a formidable leap of imagination I even convinced myself that it was the same piano.

You see, at that time, I wanted to *be* Nat King Cole. My father told me all about him and played those records until the grooves were nearly worn right through. It wasn't the ballads that got me so much, but the cookers. I was nuts for the cookers.

Of course, I never actually became Nat King Cole. This is not that kind of story. This is all for real.

My name is Foster Lutz.

My father was born in Lakeport and stayed there his whole life. My mother moved there when she was seven years old. They met on the dance floor of a long-dead nightclub when he was a carpenter and she was a seamstress. People called them beatniks because they never held on to their jobs for long and because they both loved jazz. They played me records at bedtime instead of singing me lullabies. I should have thanked them for that.

My mother was killed when I was five years old. She was crossing the street and the man driving the car that hit her drove away without stopping. I think that I could have forgiven him otherwise. Instead I lug around a hatred for somebody I've never even met. Hatred is heavy, but maybe his guilt weighs more. I used to picture the two of us standing side by side on scales, like boxers before a fight.

A couple of times a month my father would drink a lot of red wine, play records, and dance around with my mother's picture. He was big by then, clumsy, and he knocked things over. Slow dances, fast dances, he held that picture so tightly that I thought his chest would open up and take it in. Usually when he danced he would forget I was there so I'd put myself to bed.

I never went to school because in one of his short-lived jobs my father had been a teacher. Somehow he convinced the school board that he could teach me at home. Mine was an unconventional education. Mostly he played music while telling me stories about things he and my mother had done together. Things like math and spelling I learned from the textbooks we got in the mail.

We had nothing in our house that didn't belong to an age long gone, so that by the time I arrived at The Underwood in 1985 I was not exactly in touch with everything that was happening in the world. But who is?

One day when I was eight or nine my father found me in the living room listening to one of his records and playing an imaginary piano. I was singing too. I didn't notice that he was in the room until he turned down the volume.

He said to me, standing there in his boxer shorts

with a belly like a drumlin, "Foster, would you like to take music lessons? Do you want to learn to play the piano?"

I said, "Yes."

I was not going to be twenty-nine that summer; I was going to be twenty-two. I'd grown myself a sparse goatee and tried not to sleep much. For the interview I'd put on my father's crumpled fedora. I don't think I fooled anyone except for Mr. Breedle, but he was fool enough. I was where I wanted to be.

The lounge in which I stood was the same lounge I'd seen in the pictures. The same, only drunk with age. The carpet, the chairs, the walls, and the tables—they all had an elderly smell about them. It was seedy but I liked it. It was still a grand room, with thick, muscular pillars, an impressive L-shaped bar with brass rails, and massive wall-mounted mirrors that gave you an inkling of eternity no matter where you stood.

The lights were dim in the room but bright on the stage. The piano sat there, gleaming black and glorious. It was early still, and I had the place to myself. I sat on the bench and played *What's New* for a while.

I stopped playing when the bartender arrived. He looked about thirty, with short-long brown hair, ripped jeans, and a Van Halen T-shirt. His eyes were friendly in a red, squinty way that I misread as fatigue. From the look on his face I could see that he was surprised to see me sitting there at the piano.

"Who are you? Where's Lloyd?"

"He left. I'm Foster, his replacement."

"Lloyd left? Jesus, that's good. The man was a hack. Like a three-legged cat walking across the keys."

He stared off into the corner for a few seconds, allowing the departure of Lloyd to sink in, and then he turned back to me. "I'm sorry. I'm Nick. The bartender. Man you're young. When they hire you?"

"Just now."

"Huh. Well, you can't be any worse than Lloyd. Welcome . . . I guess."

"Thanks."

"I gotta get changed—the lunchtime martini crowd's gonna be here any minute." He raised a wrist and said, "Glug, glug, glug."

I watched him walk behind the bar and through a swinging door. When it stopped swinging I left the lounge, picking up my suitcase from under the table where I'd left it before the audition. It was my first suitcase. I didn't know what I'd been missing.

Everyone should have a suitcase, even if they don't go anywhere. Mine clicked open and snapped closed and held everything I owned with room to spare.

I walked up to the mahogany bulk of the front desk, squinting in the streams of sunlight that coursed through the lobby windows.

Something about the inside of the hotel made the outside hideous. Inside was cool, dark and cavernous instead of blinding, loud, and hectic. People, cars, and bicycles raced and wove around each other just outside the glass. It made me feel like sleeping.

There was no one behind the desk so I rang the bell. While I waited I looked around the room. The lobby was the most attractive part of the hotel, probably out of a faith in first impressions. The paint was fresh, pale yellow, and the carpet the crisp blue of clear skies. In the far corner four leather club chairs ringed a heavy glass table.

I rang the bell again. Still no one came so I tried calling out to Manny. When that didn't work either, I went behind the desk and helped myself to a key. I took number 136.

I rode the elevator up one floor. It groaned. The door to Room 136 was at the end of a long hallway that smelled of cigarettes. The door swung open and I stepped in. I had never stayed in a hotel room before. It didn't smell so much like cigarettes: it smelled like other people. There was a big bed with a fantastic blanket and a small table beside it. Thick red curtains blotted out the sunlight. On the wall next to the mirror there was a plaque that read 'James Cagney Stayed Here, August 10, 1953.'

I found this fact exciting. "You dirty rat," I said to the mirror.

I lay down on the bed and made a head sandwich with the pillows. And then I slept like a bear in the winter time. I didn't have to look old anymore.

When I woke the room was bruisy with shadows. The blanket had slipped down around my shoulders and I was shivering from a draught through the cracked window. I bolted up; I wasn't supposed to sleep until nightfall—I had a show to play.

I leapt out of bed and started struggling into my clothes, glancing at the clock on the wall and tripping over my pants as I did so.

But it was okay. It was only 8:00 and I wasn't on until 9:00. I stayed there on the floor, panting. There was a rugburn on my elbow from falling. I decided to get something to eat.

 My father was big on imparting wisdom. Once he told me never to eat in a restaurant that had red napkins on the table.

"Believe me Foster," he said, "it means they have something to hide. And it's too bloody bourgeois. Always go for the white napkin places. Always."

On top of the table at which I sat there was a red tablecloth and on top of that there was a red napkin folded into the shape of a crown. There were twenty tables in the dining room and maybe a dozen people scattered around them. The ceiling was high and cigarette smoke drifted up and turned blue. The four chandeliers didn't glitter so much as glow, dully. Everyone seemed to be enjoying themselves despite the sombre weight of the place. They played the happy music of restaurants.

I picked up the napkin and laid it on my lap. It just sat there, harmless as . . . a napkin. Sometimes my father talked like a crazy person.

At precisely 8:11 P.M., or a few minutes later, I fell in love. I know that it was 8:11 P.M. because I was looking at the clock when I saw her. It's the other part I'm not sure about.

There are some people who disappear inside of a uniform. The uniform is in charge; they just move it around from time to time. Then there are those who cannot be contained, and for whom fashion is irrelevant. The way she wore the black skirt and vest of The Underwood, I swear, she made them beautiful too. It was as if the clothes were smiling. Chestnut hair danced around her shoulders. She looked at me with eyes like green lighting. I took the menu from her and tried to speak. What a day I was having.

"Something to drink?"

"Yes."

She waited. "Water, maybe?"

I said, "Okay, yes, water," as if I was about to try it for the first time.

When she returned she told me that her shift was over. An ice cube popped in the water glass. She told me that Martha would be taking care of me.

I didn't want her shift to be over, but I decided not to voice this feeling. I smiled like an idiot and probably was one. She smiled back at me and then she was gone.

Martha came over a few minutes later. She wore her uniform like a sandwich board.

At 9 o'clock I stepped onto the stage. I felt stroganoff surging inside of me and my nerves were a rowdy clutch of mutineers. The spotlights seared my eyes and drew great beads of fear-scented sweat from my pores.

I had told Mr. Breedle that I was experienced—seasoned even—when in fact I'd never played in front of an audience before. I tried to pretend that they weren't there, but it was rather like pretending that your back isn't there. You don't have to look at it but it *is* there. It just is.

Mr. Breedle sat front and centre, hands folded before him on the table. His only movement was the occasional extraction of a mint from his pocket. Nick gave me a 'thumbs-up' from behind the bar and I attempted to return a confident grin. A sudden shifting of the stroganoff put a stop to the charade.

To the left of Mr. Breedle were four older women in pastel pantsuits sipping furiously at glasses of white wine and already looking disappointed. Further on a solitary man with a thick red beard was lost somewhere in a book; behind him sat a blank-faced couple who appeared to be completely oblivious of each other.

To the right several tables had been pushed together to accommodate a throng of hard-drinking businessmen. One of them had a laugh like squealing tires.

Behind them, in a shadowy corner, sat a middle-aged woman. She was waiting for someone who was obviously late, and judging from the look on her face that person would have been better off not showing up at all.

I was seated at the piano. I cleared my throat and leaned toward the microphone. The voice I heard was not my own.

"Good evening, ladies and gentlemen. My name is Foster Lutz."

The room went quiet and all eyes settled on me.

"Welcome to The Underwood Hotel. My first selection is a personal favourite. I hope you like it too. It's called *Orange Coloured Sky*."

The intro was wooden. My singing began in croaks and stutters. I kept forgetting the right time to breathe. But by the end of the song I was beginning to feel better. I became more and more relaxed as the night went on until it was almost as easy as playing in my living room. I got applause from the four women and sporadic periods of attention from the businessmen. Mr. Breedle tapped his foot. Nick whistled. By the end of the first set I was beginning to get a strange, giddy feeling almost like hunger. I didn't want the show to end.

Chapter 2

A COUPLE OF WEEKS PASSED AND I NEVER LEFT the hotel. I didn't spend much time in my room because I had the lounge to myself for most of the day. From the restaurant I got breakfast, lunch, dinner, and heart palpitations. There was nothing else I needed. The shows were going well. The first song jitters had paled and died. On the weekends more tables were full than empty. I had a home again.

One night I was in the middle of a song, making a real giddy mess of it and having the time of my life. I kept hearing this voice from the audience—this deep, heavy voice like the creaking of an old barn door. He was cut loose from the rest of them, a raw nerve, a soul too big for manners. He shouted at me, "You know it man! You know! Dig! Go, freak, go!"

At first it was distracting, but after awhile it started to egg me on. I didn't think about what my hands were doing, just closed my eyes and let them go.

It must have been ten minutes later when I wrapped it up and this guy was the only one who cheered. Everyone else was talking. He made more noise than the rest of them combined. I think he was the noisiest person I'd ever encountered.

Mr. Breedle was there in his usual seat; he craned his neck back and frowned in the direction of the racket. Then he turned around and frowned at me. I eased off after that, still feeling as if I was on a probation of sorts. I didn't want to blow it.

I'd seen this guy come in earlier with a girl about my age. He was older—thirty, at least. They were all over each other, pawing and necking like high school kids. He had a black beard and wide brown eyes. His head was shaved.

She had slender limbs, almond eyes, and a dreamy expression on her face when she watched me. His hands moved through the long dark spill of her hair like dolphins in the sea. She whistled birdsong at the end of every piece. They made it a wilderness in there.

They left before I was finished, which saddened me. Most people came for the atmosphere, for the history. It was nice to have fans. I had a feeling, though, that they'd be back.

I was half right. He came back that same night. I was getting ready to go upstairs when somebody tapped me on the shoulder.

"Baby," he said, and the barn door swung wide open. "That was hell on wheels."

The kitchen was still open and we were both hungry so we took a table in the restaurant. She was working and I blushed deep red when she took my order. She didn't seem to notice, but he did. I knew her name at that point but nothing else. Her name was Nadine. Her name *is* Nadine. Neither way sounds right.

Max watched in bemused silence as I spoke to her. When she left he punched me in the arm. I nearly fell over.

"Oh man, are you ever gone," he said, grunting laughter and shaking his head. "You should see yourself. You look like a goddamn puppydog! You think you're gonna get anywhere with that shyboy schtick?"

I stared hard at the tablecloth.

"All right, all right. So you really are a shyboy. Okay, fine."

He leaned way back in his chair and then he stopped laughing. "Listen to me—that was some dynamite you were slinging up there. Your voice is all right, but man . . . the way you play . . . I never heard anything like it. Pure sorcery."

"Thanks. It—"

"Feature this—you and me. We're gonna play together. What do you say?"

"I—what?"

"I'm talking about musical combat. We'll kill each other, dig?"

"What do you play?"

"Bull fiddle. A beauty."

"Really?"

"Really."

"All right. If you want you could come by some-time in the morning when nobody's around."

"Tomorrow. I'll be here tomorrow at eleven."

He lurched forward in the chair and drained the entirety of a fresh double scotch. He took me by my lapels. I was more or less terrified. This kind of person did not exist in my experience. Those eyes of his were crazy—they spun like roulette wheels.

"We're gonna level this shithole."

I was starting to think that Max wouldn't show up when the door burst open and he came striding in. He carried the bulk of the bass with no discernible effort. He waved it at me. I nodded back.

"Foster, man," he said. "I'm sorry I'm late. My old lady works nights at The Peepers. I don't get to see her much, you know?"

"It's all right. I was just practicing. What's The Peepers?"

"It's a club. She's a dancer."

"What about you? What do you do Max?"

He smiled and unzipped the case. "Well, Foster, I sell grass."

"What—sod?"

He stopped what he was doing and looked at me as if I'd just been replaced by someone else. "Huh? Are you putting me on? Are you for real?"

"Oh. I get it. Grass. Like dope, right?"

"That's exactly right, Foster. That's what I do."

"I thought you meant . . ."

He was walking toward the stage with the bass under his arm. His boots thumped the floor. "Yeah," he said. "I know."

Once he was up on the stage he stood there staring at me. The bass was big, but he dwarfed it. He was six-foot-five at least; neither muscular nor fat, but thick—like a tree trunk. He kept staring at me until I threw up my hands.

"What?" I said. "What?"

"Don't freak out. Where'd you get that kinky-ass hair?"

"My mom."

"Where's she live?"

"She . . . doesn't."

He slumped. "Shit. I'm sorry, man. Look how I got things started."

He ran his hands along the side of the bass and looked at the floor. I knew what he was going to say next: "You mind if I ask how?"

"She got hit by a car. Hit and run."

"Bastards. What about your old man?"

"He died too. About a month ago. Exhaust fumes."

Max dropped his head into his hands. He moaned. "Oh man . . . no more, please. I promise not to ask any more questions. Enough tragedy. I can't take it. I'm sorry for bringing it up."

"It's all right, I guess. I'm used to it."

With this he straightened up and hit a low, deep note that echoed through the hollows of the room.

"You know, Foster, if I was you I'd stay away from cars."

I hit the same note on the piano.

"I do, Max. You bet I do."

I found my father when I came home from a day of hunting through record stores. He had forgotten to open the garage door. I had a present for him under my arm. It was Count Basie. I threw it in the garbage. Sorry, Mr. Basie.

I stood there waiting for someone to come. I looked at him sitting there and decided to do something that would have made him happy. My father told me a hundred stories about The Underwood but he never did make it there himself. Playing at the hotel was the only thing I could think of to do for him. For myself, too. Paying debts to the dead is one of humanity's more peculiar traditions, but who am I to deny thousands of years of eccentricity?

Besides, there was nothing else for me to do. The bank owned the house and I wasn't about to stay there anyway. It spewed grief like chimney smoke. I hated it.

"Okay," Max said. "Lemme show you what I got. Fly me something simple."

So I put together a couple of chords, kept the pace slow, and waited for him to join in. He picked it up fast enough and his timing was right-on at first. What sunk him was flourish. He'd take off on these madman runs between the beats and we ended up tripping all over each other. If he knew this he didn't show it. We kept on until I got frustrated and stopped playing.

"Max. Uh . . ."

"Uh what? Whattaya think?"

I told him the truth. He didn't like it much.

"What? 'Tripping'? What the fuck is that supposed to mean, 'tripping'?"

"Listen Max, it's a small thing. Easy to avoid. Just don't—"

"Easy for you maybe. I . . . man, I didn't come here for lessons." He snorted and stamped his foot. "Fuck this and fuck you too, *sensei*."

I sat there and watched while he packed up. He had a hard time putting the instrument back in its case and looked as if he was going to break it—or me—in two. The only thing I could think to say was, 'Bye.' which I probably should have kept to myself. He looked at me like I was a cockroach in his clam chowder.

The door slammed behind him. I looked at the piano. "Bye," I said.

I didn't feel like playing anymore so I went out and slouched in the lobby. I thought about going after Max and apologizing but instead I stood there squinting in the daylight, watching. There were people out there: I could see them walking, talking, smoking cigarettes and holding hands. I might as well have been watching a movie.

Manny stood at his post behind the front desk. The polished buttons on his uniform glittered in the sunbeams. We'd never had a conversation but it was obvious that he didn't like me. Maybe I shouldn't have just taken that room key. It was his job, after all.

He was watching me. "What the hell are you doing?" he said.

I shrugged and went into the restaurant. Nadine was alone, sitting and smoking at one of the corner tables. She held a cup of coffee aloft as if studying its physical properties: volume, density, and weight.

She looked up when she heard me coming in. I wanted to turn around but it was too late. It was a time to be brave.

"Hey, you're the new piano player. I didn't know that before."

"Yeah. I am."

I wasn't sure what I should be doing with myself so I put my hands in my pockets and then took them out again.

"Why don't you come sit with me?"

So I sat with her. The light filtering through the gaps in the heavy velvet curtains had the odd effect of turning her hair from brown to red. I was staring.

"Are you thinking that I look different?"

"Yes."

"I dyed my hair red."

"Oh."

"Did you come in here to eat?"

"Not really."

"Bored, huh?"

I didn't say anything because it was more or less impossible to make my mouth work while I was looking at her. I think she found me amusing.

"Come on. No one's around. Let's have some cake—Devil's Chocolate. You'll like it, I promise."

The kitchen surprised me. It was large, clean, and brightly lit by banks of fluorescent lights. The counters were free of clutter—except for one of them, where the cook was asleep with his face on the cutting board. There was a bloody meat cleaver and a pile of raw chicken beside his head. He snored.

"Shhh," she said.

I eased the swinging door closed but the hinges squeaked anyway. The cook jolted up on his stool. He said, 'Balls,' then his head sunk back down and the snoring resumed.

We both laughed then and Nadine dragged me away, over to an immense silver refrigerator. Inside, there was one piece of cake left on a white plate. She took two forks from a bristling cutlery basket.

We ate the cake standing up. She was right: I did like it. Neither of us could stop laughing.

"I'm going to stick around to see you tonight. I heard you're fun to watch. Nick says when you play you look like you're getting laid."

I dropped my fork. She gave me hers. I started to fidget. "I . . . I don't know about that, but I'd like it if you came."

"You know, when you asked me my name you never told me yours. Why not?"

"I don't know. I guess I forgot."

"You forgot your name?"

"No. It's Foster."

She smiled at me. She had cake on her teeth. "Have some more, Foster."

I was about to tell her something but a wiry old man came walking through the door. He moved like a tumbleweed. There was a smile on his face that had nothing to do with where he was at that moment. He stopped and whistled when he saw us.

"Nadine," he said. "There is a customer."

Nadine said, "Oh yes, I work here," and shrugged. "Foster, this is Antoine. He's French." She put the plate into the sink and headed for the door, looking back before she went out.

"See you tonight," she said.

The door flapped back and forth after her. The

old man was still grinning, and nodding at me as if I'd just said something wise.

"So what do you do around here?"

"I am Antoine Richelieu. I am the dishwasher."

Man could that guy grin. He was pale as milk and had a small gaunt face with big eyes. He looked like a newt. I liked him. He pulled an apron off of a hook and began to tie it around his waist. I'd never seen anyone love a knot so much.

"I'm Foster. I'm the new piano player."

"I know," he said. "I know this."

The cook slipped off the stool.

I shouldn't have been surprised to see Max again. I guess I was just surprised to see him again so soon. He had on a felt hat and a look of sheepish beatitude. He came up to me before the show, shuffling his feet, eyes downcast.

"Hey," I said.

"Okay . . . okay." He held his hands up in supplication. "Don't say a fucking word. Tomorrow we'll practice again. Right? I'll listen. We'll pull it down, daddy. You with me?"

"Sure I am."

He turned to the audience and put his hand on

my shoulder. "This man is going to play for you and you're gonna clap until it hurts."

No one said a word.

I went up to the stage and took my seat. There was a good crowd that night—they were getting better every day—but I didn't know if it was me or if it was the hotel that was bringing them in. Still, I thought some faces looked familiar.

I was stretching my fingers when I saw Max go over and take the seat next to Nadine. I hadn't seen her come in. It wasn't hard to hear what he said to her over the noise of the crowd; he had that voice.

"Hello gorgeous, remember me?" He leaned closer and said something else—quietly, this time. He put his arm around her. She seemed to like it.

I played *Misty* until it bled.

They laughed and whispered through the whole set. I devised unspeakable corridors of vengeance from the stage. Through the music I promised Max blades, bullets, and boot heels. I had never been in a fight in my life but I was willing to learn. For her I was.

I finished off with a chord that made some people gasp. The legs of the bench screeched as I pushed back from the piano and began to gather up the music. The sheets fell out of my hands and scattered on the floor. I was bending down to pick them up when I smelled Mr. Breedle's minty breath over my shoulder.

"That was a little violent don't you think?"

"I guess it was. I'm sorry. I had a bad day."

"Hmmm. I'd like to speak to you tomorrow. Come to my office in the morning. Ten o'clock."

"I'll be there."

"Very good."

He turned and walked his rigid walk out into the lobby. Looking across the room I saw Max reading Nadine's palm. He made faces and she giggled. I left the music there on the floor and went over to their table. The people I passed were speaking and moving at half speed. A few of them spoke to me but I couldn't hear them over the murder on my mind. I was a cauldron of unfamiliar feelings. One of them was love and it tasted like charcoal. One of them was anger and it tasted very good indeed. My fingers started to curl up as I neared them.

They both cheered when I got there.

"I thought you were gonna kill that thing! Beautiful! The most!"

"You should be paying this guy, Foster. He's your number one fan. A bona-fide hype machine."

I stood there blinking. I think my mouth was

open. I sat down slowly and Nadine reached across the table to touch my hand.

"That was really good. I don't even like jazz usually."

Max started in on her. "What do you like? C'mon sister, tell me. I gotta know."

"I like Prince. He makes me want to dance."

"Who's Prince?" I said.

"He's kidding?"

"He's kidding. Aren't you, freak."

"Deadpan. He got me. I think I'll dance my way to the Ladies' Room."

And dance she did. I didn't say anything. My fingers straightened out again. I closed my mouth. Max's laugh shook the table.

"I know what you were thinking!"

"No you don't."

"They're gonna have to hospitalize that piano after the spanking you gave it."

"Drop it, all right?"

He put his face up close to mine and gazed as if he was looking for something inside my eyes.

"There's a beast inside you and I'm gonna get to meet him. I know he's lurking in there somewhere. Out! Out with you!"

He punched my arm and cuffed me in the head. My fingers started up again. "Leave me alone, will you?"

"Sure, I dig. You have things to do. Moves to make. And so do I. Kika's not working. It's theme night at my place. Freaky stuff, a teddy bear picnic. But I won't talk dirty talk around the likes of you."

Max started drumming on the table and stamping his feet. A few people turned toward him looking annoyed but thought better of saying anything when they saw the size of him.

"So, Foster, is there anything you want to ask me? Need any tips from the Buddha of Bedistry?"

"I'll see you later, Max."

"All right—leave you alone. I get the picture. One too many Maxes at this here table. I'll get groovin' along."

He got out of the chair and squeezed his shoulders into his leather coat. He saluted me and made for the door.

Nadine looked different when she came back. It wasn't her hair or her make-up or anything of the kind. It was more like she was sure about something that she wasn't sure about before. Her eyes swept me like headlights. She moistened her lips.

"You live here, don't you?"

"Yes."

"What's your room like?"

"It's okay. It's on the first floor so it's kind of noisy and the water cuts out sometimes but—"

"You were supposed to ask me if I wanted to see it."

I was sure that my legs would betray me but I asked her anyway. I was a passenger on this trip but it didn't bother me. It was the only way to go.

We left the table, the smoke and boozy din of the place. The last thing I heard was a man arguing with Nick. "You don't know what the hell you're talking about," he said. He sounded as if he meant it, too. Nick noticed us and stared as we went out. He looked surprised to see us together. I'll bet that I did too.

My idea of boldness was to take her hand in the elevator. Her hand was smaller and warmer than mine. When we got to my door I didn't want to let it go.

Inside, I pulled away from kissing her. It was like getting out of a warm bed in the winter dark. "Nadine. There's something I'd better tell you."

She put her finger to my lips. "I know," she said. "You have virgin written all over you."

Chapter 3

"LISTEN, MR. BREEDLE. I KNOW WHAT YOU'RE going to say, and you're right. I'm sorry I got carried away. I didn't mean to. I promise it won't happen again."

"That is not why I asked you to see me."

"Oh?"

He paused then, to let me stew. Any concern that I might lose my job had been pushed deep into the pointless corners of the previous evening. I wasn't thinking about it then—I was buried in glee. Who needs worry when you're six feet under?

But in the morning it woke me. I woke up alone. I remembered several things at once, and then I remembered my appointment with Mr. Breedle. When that came back I didn't wonder where Nadine had gone. The dread was too strong. I was unfamiliar with the elastic potential of employers. I only knew this: Without The Underwood I had nowhere to go, and nothing to do. I couldn't exactly park a piano on a street corner. I couldn't play the accordion, and I didn't have a monkey.

Mr. Breedle was tense. His moustache rippled like wheat in the wind. I noticed that his mint tray was empty, and without them he was practically sucking on his thumb. Still, he waited, and gazed at a damp patch on the ceiling as if it had designs on his person. His agenda was a mystery to me. I tried smiling but couldn't keep it up.

He sighed. "I do not want you to think that your performance last night was acceptable. It was not what I would call entertainment and it was certainly not in keeping with the traditions of this hotel. It was self-indulgent, Foster. You can leave your problems in the wings. Do you understand?"

"Yes, I do."

"Enough of that then. Shall we move on?"

"Okay."

"You should know that Lloyd came back yesterday. He came back begging for his job. *Your* job."

"He did?"

"He did."

"And?"

"And I told him that the position had been filled. Even the conventioneers knew dreck when they heard it. And he was dirty, Foster. An unclean man."

His thumb circled his mouth as he spoke. I couldn't stop watching it. "You have been doing very well for us. People have heard of you. People come to the hotel just to see you play. Did you know that you were in the newspaper?"

"What newspaper?"

"*The* newspaper, Foster. It was a favourable write-up, I might add. We—you and I—have a chance to *reinvent* The Underwood for these modern times.

"And so I think that we should consider expanding your act. Music is changing. It is vital that we continue to offer more to our clientele. More entertainment. More music."

I didn't like this new territory: it was groundless and Mr. Breedle was beginning to loom. I shifted in my chair.

"How exactly can we offer more?"

"Young man, I am prepared to use the entertainment fund to provide you with . . ."

He stopped, and his hands went up as if he was giving a sermon. He was impressing himself, but not me, not me. I had a bad feeling.

" . . . a synthesizer!"

"A what?"

"A synthesizer!"

"Ah—"

"I'm told that they can do amazing things.

Amazing. That they are expanding the frontiers of lounge music. You see, you program your accompaniment ahead of time. Ahead of *time* Foster! Be it samba, be it mambo, be it traditional jazz—you just program it and it does the—"

"No, Mr. Breedle. No."

"No? What no?"

"Hell no?"

There was more than just disappointment on his face. A darkness I had never seen in him settled upon his features. He brooded and gazed like the villains of silent films. He wanted to tie me to train tracks—I know he did. His scrap of power was dear. It was a love letter to himself.

"I don't understand you. You act as if you run this hotel. That is not so. That is not wise."

"I don't mean any disrespect sir. Look."

He looked, while I tried to think of some alternative, anything.

"All right. Okay. What if—instead of the synthesizer—I had real live musicians playing with me. Everybody loves a band. What about a trio, or a quartet maybe?"

He frowned. "That we simply could not afford."

"How much was the synthesizer going to cost?"

"It was very reasonable. Fifty dollars a month."

"Would you give me a day? Would you do that?

Please, Mr. Breedle, let me see what I can do."

He looked at his desk. He looked at the wall. Then he looked at me, and sighed. "All right. A day it is then."

I rose from the chair. "Thank—"

"Before you go there's something else, Foster. I think perhaps that it's time for you to get a new suit. The one you're wearing is beginning to look somewhat . . . peaked."

It was my father's suit. He was a good deal larger than me, and even with the tailoring I looked like a fasting scarecrow in it. I noticed that the cuffs were fraying. My shoes were his, too. I slid around in them as I went out the door.

I passed the receptionist on the stairs. She was out of breath and carried a paper bag in her hand. I didn't have to guess what was in it.

"Hurry," I said.

I went up to my room, thinking about sleep. When I got there the telephone was ringing. It had no business to ring. I could think of no one in the world who would be calling me so I ignored it. It stopped.

I crawled into the bed and took a long, deep

breath, and then I closed my eyes. Only the day before it had been an entirely different bed. I liked this one better. I thought about oceans and got caught in an undertow.

"You're late, freak."

"Yeah, I fell asleep."

The lounge was dead empty except for us. If you closed your eyes it still smelled as if it was full of people spilling drinks and sweating. The stage lights weren't on; the place was soft dark and country quiet. Max sat at one of the tables with the bulk of the bass lying across his lap. He plucked it idly, as if it were a porch guitar. He took a drag of his cigarette and studied me. The grin that lit his face cut my nonchalance into laughing pieces.

"Ho daddy! You did it, didn'tcha? You got a face like a billboard, you tramp. Tell me about it. Give!"

"Hey . . . shhh."

"Shhh nothing. Welcome to manhood you little monk bastard."

"What makes you think I never—"

"Don't do that man. Don't you insult my wisdom. You had virgin written all over you, admit it."

I hoped that I would never have to hear that again.

"So lay it out. Paint me a naughty picture."

"I don't think so."

"TELL!"

"No. We have something better to talk about, you and me."

"Better than sex? Oh man, this should be good."

"If we can get it together, you can play the shows with me."

"Get the hell out of here. What are you talking about?"

"We're going to have to practice, and I think we're going to have to find a drummer."

"Hot damn . . ."

Max looked toward the corner of the room. His face contorted and I could see him fumbling with memories. Eventually he found the one he wanted. He clapped his hands together and looked back at me.

"I know a drummer! Kevin, ahh, Kevin O' Something. He's an old buddy . . . well, not really a buddy but a customer, you dig? I think he said he played the drums. I never heard him but we'll try him out, yeah?"

"One thing. There's only fifty dollars a month. For both of you. I could maybe give you some of what I get."

"Ssst. Forget the money. Very unzen, motivation-wise. Besides, brother, I'm a man of means. I'm independently wealthy, a green tycoon. Give the fifty to Kevin. Now *he* needs it."

"Okay, then. For now let's you and me practice."

This time Max kept it simple and so did I. Did he ever know songs! He knew practically every one I threw at him. After a couple of hours it was starting to sound like the kind of music we wanted to hear. It felt good. I'm not saying it *was* good. Maybe I am.

"How do you know so many songs?"

He started laughing, leaned his bass against the wall, and sat on the edge of the stage. "The thing about what I do is—I have a lot of free time. Mostly I'm just sitting around the house, waiting for people to come around or waiting for Kika to get off work. It's a drag sometimes, real feeble.

"So I got myself a hobby—picked up this here bull fiddle. Started playing along with the records I dug. Mingus. Paul Chambers. Makes the days drift by so smooth man, so nice. But I guess sometimes I get carried away. Show off. You know."

I ran my fingers up the keys. "Max, do you smoke that stuff you sell?"

"Uh uh. It's not my party."

Kevin O' Something was not a drummer. What he played sounded like shoes in a dryer—several, heavy shoes. We tried getting him to play only the beat, but he didn't seem to get it. He was terrible. Still, Max was a bit hard on him.

Max walked over to the drum kit at the end of our second attempt at a song. His shoulders were arched high and his hands clenched into fists like sledge-heads. Strangely, his voice was softer than I'd ever heard it before.

"Kevin, you're no drummer. Why did you tell me that you were a drummer?"

Kevin said nothing.

"You get out of here now and I don't ever want to see you again. Ever. Now shake your ass out of here before I do."

"Max . . ." I said.

Kevin was not sure what was happening to him. He looked at Max with his mouth open and then he looked at the sticks in his hand.

Kevin was not entirely with us that day: he was confused when he came in and he was confused when Max introduced us. He was outright lost when he was setting up his drum kit, and when we played it looked as if someone had asked him to refute the theory of relativity—in Latin.

Kevin had long feathered hair and a phony half-smile. He wore a leather vest and tight jeans with a rolled up bandanna around his left thigh. I was not sure of the bandanna's purpose, but thought that perhaps it should be loosened a little. Whenever one of us spoke to him he laughed: a high, staccato sound that reminded me of Morse Code. He would become confused in the middle of the laugh, like he had forgotten what triggered it, and then the transmission would end. I did not like Kevin, not at all, but still, Max was a bit hard on him.

"You know something else Kevin? You still owe me three hundred fucking dollars and until I get it you're going to leave that drum kit right where it's standing. Sticks and all. Now, go."

Max aimed a meaty hand at the door.

Kevin said, "What?" and a laugh leaked out of him.

I winced, and watched as Max stepped behind the drum kit and put his hands on Kevin's shoulders. "Kevin," he said. He almost looked sad.

Kevin laughed again, and tried to crane his neck around to look at Max's face. Max picked him up as if he was a bag of dirty laundry and carried him to the door. Kevin laughed the whole way. When they reached the door Max threw him out, just like that. Kevin's head knocked against the thick wood and I cringed with the hollow sound of it.

Max took his time coming back to the stage. He stopped and lit a cigarette, then went over to the bar to pour himself a glass of water. I just sat there watching him, silent.

When he climbed back up onto the stage he picked up the bass and started into a song I didn't recognize. Then he stopped, and looked at me. When he did it was like the past hour had never happened. His eyes were bright.

"So. I guess we still need a drummer, huh freak?"

"I guess we do."

"Antoine," she said.

"What about Antoine?"

"Antoine's a drummer. He used to be, anyway. He played here for years. When things died down he stuck around and started washing dishes. He likes it here."

We were lying in my bed in the middle of the afternoon. It had been a week since that first night and I couldn't get enough of Nadine. The curtains were drawn tight and I could barely see her through the shadows. I wanted to, so I reached over her and clicked on the light. She ducked under the covers.

"I don't know, Nadine. Antoine is very old."

Her voice was muffled: "I'm just saying. He's a drummer. And you need one."

"Does he still play?"

"Foster! He's downstairs. Ask him. He's a nice man. I'm going to sleep before my shift starts."

So I went.

I found Antoine stooped over the yawning sink in a shroud of steam. It was a slow time of day, and there was no one else in the kitchen, just him and me. He held onto the spray nozzle at the end of a long translucent hose, directing a jet of scalding water at greasy pots and pans. He was hypnotized. He danced with the hose, teasing and easing like a snake charmer.

"Antoine?"

He couldn't hear me through the steam. There was a skillet in the sink with some charred substance caked to the bottom. He worked at it with the nozzle and a brush, turning his head to and fro and whispering something that I couldn't understand. Little by little he worked it clean. He smiled.

"Antoine?" I reached out and touched his shoulder. His head rotated slowly in my direction. He looked toward me, but not at me. He was somewhere else, and it seemed like a good place to be. There was old joy in his eyes.

"Hello Antoine."

"Well. Allo there, piano man . . ."

His accent sounded thick in his mouth, like food.

"Can you take a break? Just for a minute? There's something I want to talk to you about."

He glanced around the deserted kitchen and shrugged. "Do you make a joke? I can take a break. Where do we go fella?"

"The lounge."

He dropped the hose.

"Aha," he said.

He walked up close to the stage, then stood there gazing dreamily at the drums. His hands started to move where they hung, tapping on the fabric of his baggy wool pants.

He spoke with wonder: "*Regard*."

"You like them?"

"But from where did they come? For how long have they been here?"

"Not long. You play? Nadine says you used to play."

"Yes, yes . . ."

The whole time we spoke he kept staring at the drums. He could have been looking at a lost love from the window of a moving bus. His eyes were wet.

"Who did you play with up there?"

"Oh many, many people. Everyone. In those days this hotel . . . it was a different place."

"You came here from France?"

"Of course."

I swept my hand toward the drum kit, nudged him a little, and said, "Maybe you'd like to try them out. See how it feels."

Antoine shuffled up to the stage without answering. He took a pair of glasses out of his shirt pocket and put them on. He was still wearing his apron.

I took a seat at one of the front tables and watched him circle the drums, touching a cymbal with the tip of his finger, rapping on the snare with a knuckle, twisting the stool, and then taking up the sticks in his hands. He waved them in the air, like wands. I still didn't know if he could play, but watching him was like watching clouds and I was entranced.

He sat down on the stool and held the sticks out for a long time without moving. He brushed one against a cymbal. Then he began to click it against the rim of the snare. The thud of the bass drum almost seemed to startle him.

And then, little by little, I began to notice a rhythm. It was tentative at first, meek even, but then it was as if he forgot that he had forgotten. It was urgent, then flailing, then steady, then soft. He was rusty but he wasn't going to stay that way.

I was just beginning to think that Antoine might work out all right when something in him seemed to snap into place, like a puzzle piece. He started killing that drum kit. There was age in the sound of it but it didn't hold him back.

It reminded me of someone else. I couldn't place it at first, but then it came to me: on the outside he was a quiet, slow old man, but on the inside, no.

On the inside he was Buddy Rich, a screaming fiend.

Antoine stopped playing. He was breathing hard and grinning awe. He stood up and came over to me.

"Piano man, I did not think that this thing was still inside of me. It makes me happy. We will play together, yes?"

"Yes, we will."

"I must leave you now. I must see my love."

He left me sitting there. Who was I to stop him?

"Antoine, do you know *Caravan*?"

He waved his sticks at me. "Play. Play."

We played. It was our last practice before the trio premiered, and I loved the way it sounded. So did Max—I could tell. He kept looking at Antoine as if he had sunlight streaming out of his pockets. We'd been at it every day for over a week, although it felt to me as if we were ready after the second day. There were plenty of songs that all three us could play by memory, and we even started working on some of our own.

Antoine stopped us in the middle of a song and both Max and I looked over at him to see what was the matter. He looked back at us, from one to the other.

"How do you say . . ." He frowned. "It is not . . . right. Songs do not go chop, chop, chop. They live, my boys. You understand me?"

"Not exactly," I said.

"Me neither."

"Ahhh. *Comme un coeur*. A . . . heart, yes? Not always the same but more fast when you feel things. We are three but we must feel things together."

"Okay," Max said, grinning.

"I think I know what you mean," I said.

I was beginning to, anyway.

We were about to start another song when Max held us up. It was obvious that he had something on his mind: obvious to me from the second he'd walked into the lounge. He was never good at hiding things.

"Hey, Foster?"

"Uh huh?"

"There's something I wanna ask you."

"So, ask."

"Well . . ."

"Well what?"

"It's just that I was gonna make up some posters. For the band, dig? And . . ." He looked at Antoine. Antoine looked at his fingernails.

"It's about your name."

"What about my name? What?"

"Well, you know, 'The Foster Lutz Trio'—it doesn't really ring. It's more like a thud. No offense, man, but *ouch*. Maybe we could change it for, like, publicity purposes."

"You want me to change my name."

He waved me off. "Just for the poster—that's it. Feature this—'The Foster Lewis Trio'. Yeah? Is that the most or what? Now *that* rings. I can see album covers with that name. Lutz, not so much."

I could never explain my reason to him, but it was never going to happen. I had a purpose above and beyond the consideration of publicity. I had a debt, of sorts. I was a Lutz.

"Max, no."

He took it well. He never mentioned it again. Sometimes I marveled at the fact that he ever listened to me. I wouldn't have. Lutz is a real clunker of a name.

Antoine didn't want to play anymore and both Max and I were hungry so we packed it up for the day. As Antoine went out I noticed that he was sweating and shaking a little. He went out of the lounge on unsteady legs.

As we walked into the restaurant Max said, "Are we killing the old guy? Is it too much for him? Is he sick or what?"

"I don't know. I watch him. It comes and goes."

"I wish it would go for good."

"Yeah."

"Man—this place is bleak. You wanna eat somewhere else? Chinese maybe?"

"No. I like it here."

We were sitting at the bar—Max, Antoine, and I—watching the lounge fill up. It was a good crowd for a week night, and the usual batch of tourists and hardcore drinkers was beefed up by some rowdy college students and an obviously wealthy, lamp-bronzed couple who wore matching clothes.

Max was nervous, I think. He kept drinking Heinekens and looking at his watch. Antoine looked at his reflection in the mirror behind the bar. He was fascinated by it. From time to time he'd reach up and touch the skin on his face, pulling on it to take away the wrinkles. He was looking much better than he had been earlier, and he had that grin screwed back on tight.

"Foster."

I turned in the direction of the voice and found Nick standing there in front of me. He was in a bad mood—I could tell by the way he was standing. He took a jerky swallow of beer and then wiped his mouth. His teeth were bared a little, and he leaned closer to speak to me.

"Let me buy you a drink."

"I don't drink Nick. You know that."

He shook his head and his look got sharper. "All right. So you don't want to accept my hospitality. That's fine. But you better let me give you some advice. I think you need it."

"Advice?"

"Yes."

"Well?"

"You've been spending some time with Nadine."

"I have."

"Well—it's none of my business, I know, but I

thought I'd do you a favour and let you in on something."

Max tuned into the conversation then, looking back and forth from Nick to me. Nick leaned even closer to me and whispered what he said next. He smelled like cheese. I didn't like him anymore.

"You seem like a guy who hasn't, you know, been around too much. I'm not saying this to insult you, Foster. It's just the way I see things. Believe me, in this job I've learned to read people pretty good."

Nick seemed to want me to respond to this but I didn't know how so I sat there, waiting. I could hear Nick's breathing; it was fast and shallow.

"So you haven't been around too much but you should know that Nadine has. She's been everywhere, you get me? Didn't it seem kind of . . . easy?"

"Whoa," Max said.

The punch I threw was not a fierce one—it was my first, after all—but it was hard enough to knock Nick back a couple of steps. The bottles rattled when he bumped the bar, and then his eyes flared like match-heads. I had no idea what would happen next. I looked at Max who looked at Nick who was still looking at me.

He hissed: "I was trying to help you, you little prick. You're gonna wish you'd listened when she's through with you."

He went down to the other end of the bar and rubbed his jaw. I rubbed my hand and couldn't stop blinking. Max slid off of his stool and began to jump up and down.

"THE MONSTER! I SAW THE MONSTER! IT LIVES! IT LIVES!"

He grabbed hold of me and tried to make me dance with him. I tried to shake him off but it was like wrestling a grizzly bear with opposable thumbs. Finally I freed myself, and stood there shaking, overwhelmed.

Antoine seemed to think that the commotion was coming from inside of his head; he peered into his water glass as if a means of restoring peace was floating in there.

I felt half mad and half sick. The sick half was taking over with every passing second.

Max calmed down. "Foster, are you all right?"

"Fine. Just . . . tense."

Down the bar Nick glared at me as he poured white wine for a man in red suspenders. I turned away from them and went into the restaurant.

Nadine was in the midst of serving a herd of starving Shriners. I could tell they were starving by the way they were sitting: backs straight, utensils at the ready, red napkins on their laps, and red hats tilted forward. But every time she set down a plate they said, "Oh," as if what was placed before them was not Chicken Cordon Bleu, Beef Stroganoff, or Sole in Lemon Cream Sauce, but in fact a heaped up, steaming plate of excrement. When they saw their food they slumped. I didn't get it.

I took Nadine by the arm and dragged her into the kitchen. She didn't seem particularly surprised by my behaviour. She never was, never once. The Shriners were, though: you should have seen their faces.

The three cooks were hard at work in the kitchen; it smelled of onions, meat, and smoke. They were three stocky, dark haired men, and each had a broad face, red from the heat. They could have been brothers. They didn't look up as we went past them, back into the quiet of the pantry. They chopped, grilled, and stirred. What they were doing was important to them.

I shut the door of the pantry behind us. The shelves were stocked high with cans and boxes: fruit, vegetables, coffee beans, bread and pasta in no sensible order. A box of ripe tomatoes sat on the floor.

I put my arms around her and my mouth on hers. Her eyes closed and I closed mine. Before long I lost track of where we were; it just felt like we were going

down, down under the floorboards with the pipes
and the wires.

When I came out of the pantry I had tomato
juice in my hair and on my skin. I liked the feel
of it. I went out of the restaurant and into the lounge.
Max and Antoine saw me coming; they got up from
the bar and we three took the stage. The posters had
worked: The Underwood was jammed tight. I was so
flushed that I forgot to introduce us. Antoine clicked
his sticks together and we just started playing.

That night I too saw the monster. The piano
quivered and breathed. The black wood laid out
before me was skin stretched tight. The keys were
pumping veins, the pedals muscle and tendon, and
the strings singing nerves. Through my fingers I felt
the beating of a heart, a quickened, lunatic pulse
that merged with my own and rearranged my insides
like some good poison.

We shook the dust from the cracks of The
Underwood. Dust rained on us—it rained on everything. We soared. We dove. We lit up like fireworks.
We settled down like night. We were the puppeteers
of the cosmos—the sound of things made and the
sound of things destroyed. We charged at outraged

ghosts and dredged up unborn souls. Every song was a living thing, like Antoine said, and everyone in the audience our rapturous hostage.

At least it felt that way to me.

CHAPTER 4

IN MY DREAM THE STREETS WERE SEETHING WITH cars. I stood on the sidewalk, alone, watching them. It was raining from a blue sky. I wasn't sure if I was myself or someone else because I couldn't see my feet. How are you supposed to know who you are if you can't see your feet?

The cars went fast. They raged through the streets, their tires squealing and crying. There were no drivers that I could see. The cars were out having a good time by themselves.

And then, one by one, they began to run into things. Everything. They crashed through storefront windows and thick shards of plate glass burst out into the streets. They crushed walls of brick and felled telephone poles with lumberjack grace. They rammed the foundations of skyscrapers and tore up long swaths of asphalt.

And then they noticed me.

I woke up. It was past noon; I could tell by the way the sun lit the curtains. There was someone pounding on my door. I stumbled bleary-eyed and senseless out of bed and went to open it. It was Max. He was standing against the opposite wall, rubbing the baldness of his head and actually sobbing. I thought I was still dreaming.

"What? What's happening?"

"Lemme in willya?"

I stood aside and he shuffled in, sat on the bed, then lay down and curled up. I sat on the dresser and looked at him. His eyes were red from crying; he sniffed, sighed, and continued to rub his head.

"So?"

"Kika left."

"Oh. Sorry Max, I—"

"I can't believe it. Yesterday I come home and all her stuff's just gone. I thought I was in the wrong apartment. I don't get it. We had kicks, man, it was holy. What was wrong? She never said anything."

I wanted to help him but I didn't know how. He sat up on the bed a little, propping himself against the wall, but he kept his eyes on the blanket. The bed sagged beneath him.

"So then . . . so then I go to the place she works, you know, to see her. Her boss—this fucking greaseball in a leather suit—he tells me how she quit the day before. And dig this: she took off with some cop who kept coming in to see her. You believe that shit?"

He shook his head, sniffed again, and looked up at me. "Man. Talk about insult and injury. A god-damn cop, goddamn it. What is it with cops and strip clubs anyway? They're all perverts. All of 'em."

"Kika was a stripper?"

He stared at me, sitting up some more. "I told you that. Don't you remember?"

"You said she was a dancer. I thought she was just a dancer."

Max allowed himself to chuckle. The chuckle took hold and wouldn't let go, and soon enough he was rolling around on the bed, howling and holding on to his guts as if he thought they were going to fall out. He laughed so hard that even I thought they might fall out.

"You're too much! What did you think she was? A tap dancer? A ballerina? Some day I wanna see the rock you've been living under. Promise you'll take me there, freak. Promise."

"I thought she was in a show or something."

"A 'show,' he says. *Oklahoma*! *My Fair Lady*! Too much."

Max sat up on the bed and grinned. My particular brand of dumb was the best thing for the occasion, it seemed. He pulled a checkered handkerchief out of his pocket, wiped his eyes and blew his nose.

"Foster, man, I've gotta tell you. You're the best friend I ever had. You're a gas."

"Have you been drinking?"

"Yeah, but . . . look, I'm not going sappy on you or anything."

"I think you are."

He froze. "What? What did you just say?"

Then he jumped up from the bed, knocked me off the dresser and put me into a headlock. I'd never been in a headlock before. There's nothing at all you can do about it. Once it's on you, you just have to be patient. If you fight it you'll go crazy.

Finally he let me go and sat back down on the bed. I could tell he was going to start crying again.

"Goddamn. I miss her already."

But I was getting ahead of myself there. Things happened between the night we first played and the day that Kika left Max for a pervert cop. Many things happened, a month of things. They happened so fast that I can take no responsibility for them. These things, they had a mind of their own.

The word was out. People came to see us: people

bored to desperation with the confectionery drone of pop radio. They wanted something different, and, for whatever reason, we were it. There weren't thousands of these people, but there were enough to fill the lounge almost every night we played. We flourished.

I wasn't singing as much anymore because it took away from this thing that the three of us had, which was growing all the time. But we held onto a few numbers: mostly the cookers that everyone loved so much.

Antoine had missed a couple of nights. He never told us where he'd been and we learned quickly enough not to bother asking. We didn't even know where he lived. He'd show up in the afternoon to wash the dishes and then he'd leave. He'd come back to play with us, or he wouldn't. We sounded all right without him but it wasn't the same. He could set us up or bowl us over with the flick of a wrist. We loved it.

He seemed to like playing with us so we both figured that he had some other responsibility that wasn't our business. When he was around he was good for our morale: he had this way of being entertaining even when he was staring at the floor, which he did a lot. Maybe he got wisdom from floors. Why not? A floor can say as much as a book if you look at it for long enough.

During this time Nadine went home to visit her family. I was a simpering wreck without her. I couldn't concentrate on books, couldn't listen to the radio; all food tasted like oatmeal and every morning broke like tragedy. I played the piano all day, sort of. I sat in front of it anyway, moping.

Nadine's family lived in the country—just outside of a small town called Wooster. They had a huge farm and their own grain elevator. You could see the grain elevator for miles and miles. It was the king of the land.

She told me that the shadow of that grain elevator used to follow her wherever she went in their yard. She couldn't get away from it her whole life. I found that hard to believe. She'd come to the city, after all.

"But all these buildings around here are the same thing," she said. "Why do people have to make things so big?"

I had no answer for her.

The three of us sat in the restaurant. We were killing time before the show, fueling up and watching the other diners pay their bills and head into the lounge. Max had something in his beard and a spot of spilled beer on his shirt. He spoke with his mouth full, quickly and without stopping. Antoine sat there, not eating, half-listening. I picked at my oatmeal-tasting food and tried to keep up with whatever Max was on about.

"Hey. You see that movie on TV last night? The late movie?"

"I don't watch TV."

"You what? You don't watch TV?"

"No. I never had one until I came here. I don't even know how to work it."

"So what the hell do you do up there?"

"I don't know."

Max set down his cutlery, wiped his beard and put his hands together. "Right. Don't lose it on us now, Foster. Listen to me: TV will keep you sane. It's your friend when you're alone. When you're not alone, and things aren't going so well, TV is your middle man. Something to talk about, you know? Give it a try sometime—it can do amazing things. It might even loosen up your freaky upstairs a little."

"My upstairs?"

"What the hell was I talking about? You made me forget." He scratched the gleaming baldness of his head.

"A movie."

"Oh yeah. A great old movie, this one. I didn't

catch the title. Paul Newman and Sidney Poitier playing jazz in Paris. They meet some chicks and walk around and blow their horns like crazy. Ahhh. What was—"

"It's called *Paris Blues*."

"Aha! How do you know that if you don't watch TV?"

"My father used to take me to this theatre that showed old movies. We saw that one twice. Louis Armstrong's in it too."

"Yeah! That's it. That's the one. You ever play with Louis Armstrong, Antoine?"

"Pardon?"

"Louis Armstrong. Did you ever play with him?"

"Ahhh. Yes. I think that I played with him. There was a man who looked like Louis Armstrong. The sound of his trumpet was like Louis Armstrong also. He did not say his name. I was in France. A boy."

Max drained his glass of beer and thumped the table. He looked at Antoine and then at me. I was afraid that Max had been thinking. He was my friend, but I didn't like it when he did that.

"Okay. I've been thinking. Feature this—the three of us in Paris. We hang there for a while, have some kicks, see what happens. You know—play the clubs, see the sights, drink wine, eat better food than this slop—we live it up French-style, dig? This town's getting to be a drag on me. If I have to meet one more fucking lawyer at his tennis club I'm gonna jump out a window."

I could think of several sturdy reasons that I did not want to go to Paris, but instead of giving them voice I said, "I don't know, Max."

"Yeah, yeah. Don't tell me. You like it here, right? You like it here too goddamn much. You gotta get out and see the world in this life. Get in touch with your inner hobo. You don't even leave this hotel. You even know what's next door to this place?"

"I . . ."

"And don't worry about Nadine. She'll be around. Hell, we could even take her with us, like a manager or something. Help me out Antoine, you wanna go back to the motherland doncha?"

Antoine blinked a few times and then a stern dark look came over him. It was the closest thing to anger I'd ever seen him show. He took a long breath.

"No. Paris is no good. There are rats. The rats are everywhere in Paris."

"Rats?"

"Rats of a terrible size. You could not imagine these rats. My friend, Gilles, he was a guitar player. One night he drank many glasses of whisky and he fell in the street. His head was sick—no, hurt. No people were in the street because of the hour. A rat chewed from his hand and he did not wake. And then he could not play the guitar."

Max laughed. "Come on, old man. That never happened."

"It happened. I tell you that it happened."

"But we got rats here too. Rats are everywhere."

Antoine sighed and beckoned us closer. We leaned forward in our chairs. He put his right hand on Max's shoulder and his left hand on mine.

"Boys. Listen well. The rats here are not rats. They are nothing. Mice. The rats of Paris come from another time. They are *anciens*. They have souls, like you and I. The rats of Paris, they speak to you."

Max and I said, "They speak to you?"

"With the eyes, with the eyes."

He took his hands from us and pulled on his face so that his own eyes opened wide, impossibly wide. They were yellow around the edges like old paper. He leaned so close that I thought I could hear his heartbeat.

"Piano man, do you know what they say?"

I swallowed. "No."

"They say, *I know you, and I know how to hurt you*."

Max laughed. "Cut it out, you're scaring the boy."

He was.

"And there's no such thing as a talking rat. I don't believe a word you say, old man."

"Foster, Max—I would not lie to you for anything."

So much for Paris.

"Thank you very much for coming to The Underwood, ladies and gentlemen. On the bass—Maxwell Brunt. On the drums—Antoine 'Buddy' Richelieu. My name is Foster Lutz. Good night."

We'd played later than usual, and because it was a week night people were putting on their coats and heading for the door before we even stepped off the stage. The lights came up; Antoine made for the restroom and Max for the bar. I was standing just off the stage, not sure what I wanted to do with myself, when I saw a man approaching me.

He had silver hair, wore a brown trench coat, and had a notepad in his hand. He introduced himself as Albert Fitzmaurice, jazz critic for *The Journal*. He said it just like that: "I'm Albert Fitzmaurice, jazz critic for *The Journal*." We shook hands.

"I enjoyed your performance very much. It was wonderful, wonderful. And quite the pair of side men you have there."

"Side men?"

"I'd like to write a piece about you for the Sunday Edition. How would you feel about answering a few quick questions?"

"Maybe you should talk to Max, the bass player. He's sort of the mouthpiece of the band." My eyes scanned the room and found him engaged in frantic kisses with a woman over by the bar. I looked closer. It was Kika.

Albert was looking too. "It seems as though your bass player is busy, Foster. And besides, it is your group isn't it? It says so on the sign outside the hotel."

"It does?"

"Why . . . yes. Let's go have a seat, shall we?"

Before we sat Albert asked if he could buy me a drink. I took a chair and waited as he went to the bar. He had to stand beside Max and Kika. It was obvious that the two of them made him uncomfortable. I might have been uncomfortable too: it looked as if they were eating each other alive.

As Nick poured my ginger ale he glared across the bar at them, and then he glared across the room at me. We hadn't spoken since I took my swing at him. I wasn't saddened by this rift.

Albert returned with the drinks. His was white wine. Max always said that the wine at The Underwood tasted like feet but Albert didn't seem to notice. He took a meager sip from the glass and then swished the wine around in his mouth.

"All right then. To begin. How old is Foster Lutz?"

"I'm twenty-one."

I flinched when I told him my real age because Mr. Breedle was a voracious reader of newspapers. My lie was back again. See what happens when you tell a lie? It never stops trailing you.

"And how long have you been playing the piano?"

"I started when I was eight, I think."

"Who taught you to play jazz?"

"I took lessons on the piano for a while. Jazz I picked up from records."

He asked me where I came from, who my influences were, and in what direction I wanted to go, musically speaking. I told him that I was happy right where I was.

"Well, this must be a dream come true for you then."

"Sort of."

I looked around the lounge. The last stragglers were finishing their drinks, butting their cigarettes, and filing out. Max took Kika's hand and led her away. She was crying.

Antoine was gone, too. I wanted to go. Albert sipped at his wine and jotted down a few lines. I couldn't read them, and wondered why he was writing when I wasn't talking. I hoped that he couldn't read minds because I was thinking about how bored I was.

"Foster, how would you define jazz?"

"How would I—"

"Yes. Define for me what it is that you do up there."

"I don't know. I never thought about it that way."

Albert Fitzmaurice was surprised. "But this is what you do every day. You must think about it. What will I write? People want to know what your ideas are, Foster."

I sighed. I couldn't talk anymore. "Make something up," I said.

I excused myself from the table and thanked him for coming. We shook hands, and he frowned at me as I turned toward the door. Upstairs, the empty room let me in without any questions.

That Sunday I opened the newspaper and found the column by Albert Fitzmaurice. I thought that he might have decided to write about someone else after the rudeness of my exit but there it was: a tidy appraisal of our performance with a few words from yours truly at the end.

This was my definition: "A fusion of technique and emotion. A boundless journey into the very idea of music."

What the hell was I talking about?

"I'm back."

"Who are you and why are you in my room?"

Nadine hit me in the stomach. I wasn't prepared and sank to the floor, wheezing. She pulled me up onto the bed and kissed me.

"Ouch."

"You don't take a punch very well."

"I guess I don't."

She got up, walked out of the room, and closed the door behind her. It was morning, a forever after she'd left, and I'd been starting to wonder if she was ever coming back. I was also starting to wonder why she'd left again already. The door opened.

"I'm back."

"I'm so happy I could throw up."

"That's better."

Later on we lay in bed listening to the traffic noise outside my window. She was stretched out on her stomach, undressed, playing with her hair and whistling. I watched her.

Nadine's trip home was depressing. Her parents didn't like the idea of her living in the city. They both agreed on this issue, but for some reason argued with each other over it while she sat there and listened. Her younger sisters asked her too many questions about too many things. Their German Shepherd had developed serious intestinal problems. He moped around the house whimpering and dragging noxious fumes behind him like an extension of his tail. She was glad to be back.

Nadine rolled over and looked at me. "Oh, by the way, I bumped into Max when I got back to town."

"Oh."

"I'm having him and his girlfriend over for dinner tomorrow night before the show."

"Uh huh."

"Don't 'uh huh' me buddy. You're coming."

"I can't. Got some things to do around here. You know, loose ends."

She got out of bed and began to walk around the room. There was nothing in it of mine—nothing visible, anyway—and it was to this nothing that she motioned as she spoke: "What loose ends? The only loose ends around here are coming out of your head. Don't you want to see where I live?"

The truth was that I had never thought about

where she lived. I knew she had to live somewhere, that outside of The Underwood there was a place where she slept, changed her clothes, took showers, and made breakfast; but this somewhere never got beyond a vague notion in my head. It was somewhere else, that was all. I decided not to answer her.

"You're coming."

"I'd rather not. I'm tired."

"You're already tired for tomorrow? How does that work?"

"I—"

"If you don't come you'll never have me in this room again. Get it?"

It was difficult to argue with her when she was naked. And so it was as simple as that. I was going outside. It had become an alien thing, like a black hole or a place called Club Med that I kept hearing about. I knew that it existed but it had nothing to do with me. I didn't even know what season it was.

I had found my way to The Underwood once. All I had to do was find my way back. It wasn't going anywhere. The streets are friendly, I told myself. Friendly streets with friendly people.

The telephone began to ring. I closed my eyes and thought about the next day.

"Do you want me to answer it?"

"No. It's not for me."

CHAPTER 5

O UTSIDE, IT WAS SUMMER. OF COURSE IT WAS.
It was 5 o'clock in the afternoon and I was
standing in front of The Underwood, blinking in
the sunshine. It felt as though, in my exile, the sun
had moved closer to the earth, nuzzling up to it like
an unwanted admirer. When I first emerged I saw
only spots, but then the spots resolved themselves
into trees, birds, buildings, and a woman in a torn
wedding dress screaming at the shade.

As I took a deep breath to fortify myself a dumptruck groaned by and belched black smoke in my
direction. The side of the dumptruck read: 'Carbon
City Municipal Works.' It was followed by a red
sports car that seemed to have all the music in the
world screaming out of its tinted windows.

I looked at the map in my hand. Nadine had
drawn it up for me that morning. She said, "Any idiot
in the world could follow this, so you should be okay."

It was neat and detailed and I had great faith in it as my co-pilot. It told me that I should rotate to the right and walk three blocks.

The street upon which I stood was called 'Cartwright.' I remembered that from when I'd first arrived at The Underwood with my treasured suitcase in my hand. I looked behind me. The hotel was small on the outside. I was puzzled by the fact that something so small could hold so much. I rotated to the right and began to walk.

On the third block of Cartwright I was so busy reading the map that I almost bumped into a man in an army uniform. We both stopped in our tracks, facing each other, nose to nose. We both stepped to the left, to the right, and then back to the left again. I started to laugh, and then he did too.

He stepped around me and disappeared down the street. I watched him go; I was in no hurry.

It wasn't so bad outside. I liked the smell of the air and the sound of things happening around me. I went onto the street called 'Bailey' and turned left with the map flapping in my hand.

All that I knew of the city was my short trip from the bus station to the hotel, so everything was new to me. There were nice houses there: aged wood and ancient brick; porches and staircases; every colour I'd ever seen and a few I hadn't.

Before long I was standing in front of '16 Ladner Street,' which was the same address that was written on the map. I wanted to keep walking. I could hardly believe it.

It was a good-looking three-storey building, freshly painted white, with balconies and ivy climbing all over a high lattice fence. I mounted the steps, went through the front door, and found my way to Apartment 2.

The hallway smelled like forty different kinds of cooking. The best smelling kind was coming from right in front of me. I knocked.

Max stood up when he saw me. "Now this I can't believe. Would you just look at him? Our little boy's all growed up!"

"Hi," Kika said. "Remember me?"

They were sitting around Nadine's dining table with glasses of wine and water. Nadine came over and hugged me.

"Unbelievable," she said, and then went back to finish cooking.

"That smells good."

Max said, "Damn. I never thought I'd see the day. And you got here on your own two legs. Were you scared, freak? Was it terrible?"

"It was okay."

Max put his arm around Kika and squeezed her. "Look who's back!" She had a shy smile.

I didn't ask what happened to the cop; I figured it was probably the wrong thing to do. Instead I looked around at Nadine's apartment. Now that I was there, I was curious.

It was small but bright, and the ceilings were high. Plants everywhere. There was a dresser, an overflowing bookshelf, and a big bed in the far corner behind a lace curtain. I thought that I could probably sleep in it if she asked me.

There were paintings on the walls and on the hardwood floor. An unfinished one sat on an easel near the bed. Most of the paintings were of farmhouses, or farmland, or barns. One was of the German Shepherd in happier times.

A brown grain elevator figured in almost all the paintings. Sometimes you could only see the base of it, and sometimes it was off in the distance, lurking around the horizon like the stranger children aren't supposed to talk to. I shivered.

Nadine came back with a pot of steaming pasta in tomato sauce and she set it down on the table beside a bowl of tossed green salad. I went to sit down; the walking had made me hungry.

We ate and talked until it was time to go back to The Underwood for the show. Kika and Max were careful around each other. We were careful around them too. I could tell that they wanted to finish each other's sentences sometimes, but they always checked themselves before they spoke.

On the way back to the hotel we stopped to buy double scoop waffle cones. I was almost reluctant to go back. Kika and Max strolled ahead of us as we walked down Cartwright. I turned to Nadine.

"Hey," I said. "Did you paint all those paintings back there?"

"I did."

"I liked them. I see what you mean about the grain elevator. How come you never told me you were a painter?"

"I don't know. They're just things I remember."

"Would you give me one for my room?"

She licked her ice cream cone and put her arm around my waist. "When you come back you can take any painting you want."

We kept walking along for a while, not saying anything. At the door of The Underwood Nadine whispered in my ear, "Do you want to sleep in my bed tonight?"

"Okay," I said.

It was a good day, but the night rebelled. Antoine didn't show up. When I sang, my voice sounded like a rusty squeezebox. Max and I played as if we were in different time zones and the songs didn't end so much as expire. The audience went about their business as if we weren't even there.

I kept hearing a small man at one of the front tables saying to the large woman beside him, "Let's get out of here. Let's get out of here."

I wished they would. I wished they all would, and I got my wish. The small man and large woman started a trend. By the time we gave up there was hardly anyone left besides Nadine, Kika, and Mr. Breedle. Even they looked bored. Mr. Breedle had taken up cigarettes again, and was puffing so hard by the end that I could hardly see him through his smoke. When we finished he stood, shook his head, and walked out without a word. The only one who appeared to have enjoyed the show was Nick.

Max took his bass, went over to Kika, and then they too left without saying anything. Something had gone wrong—I should have stayed inside.

So I was not in the kind of mood that I wanted to be in the first time I slept in Nadine's bed, but I was in that kind of mood anyway. It was stronger than I was.

I sulked as we walked down Cartwright, brooded

my way down Bailey, and moped along Ladner. What fun I must have been.

"So you had a bad night."

"Uh huh."

"Can I help you?"

"Nope."

We got into her bed and she rolled over onto her side, facing the wall. I couldn't tell if she was sleeping but kind of hoped that she was. I lay beside her staring at the ceiling, watching the fan turn around and around. After a while I got up and put on my clothes. I went back to The Underwood, and forgot to take a painting.

"Hello Antoine."

"Mighty fucking decent of you to join us."

Max and I were warming up the night after our disaster. We were about as mad as we could be at Antoine, upon whom we had placed all the blame for what had happened. We both glared at him but he didn't notice. He was above such things, or below them—I could never tell which. He stood there in his rumpled tweed suit and looked at the drum kit.

"What do we play tonight?"

"What happened to you? Where were you?"

"Yeah, old man. You too good for us or what? You got something else going on?"

Antoine got up on stage and sat down at the drums. He picked up the sticks and started playing. We tried to keep at him over the noise but he couldn't hear us so we just joined in.

That night he was in charge. Max and I were still sapped of confidence from the night before, so Antoine led the way. We just loped along behind him, trying to keep up. It was impossible to remain angry at him because he saved us from another night of torture. Midway through the second set he had us chugging along as good as ever.

I noticed the man with the grenade long before I knew that he had it there in the pocket of his greasy raincoat. I'd never seen him in the hotel before, and without exchanging a word or a look I knew I never wanted to see him again.

He was shifty: in his eyes, his posture, and in the way he held a glass. He sat at one of the middle tables and drank a lot and the look on his face went from mildly unpleasant to mean, then well beyond into the bleak terrain of the downright nasty. Then he started yelling at us as we finished a song.

"Play *All of Me*," was what he yelled. "Play *All of Me*, goddamn you!"

We ignored him and played *Route 66* instead. Now, *Route 66* is one of the happiest songs ever written. It beats up blues, breaks up fights, and has probably prevented a suicide or two. Even to a barnacle like me it gave a sweet taste of the freedom of the road—the urge to drive west and hunt down the sun.

This man sneered. The sneer contorted his face into a new degree of sinister. Max was just beginning his solo when the man yelled it again. But this time it sounded more like a bark than a yell—a *command*.

Max stopped playing and leaned over his bass. For a moment he looked even meaner than the man he was talking to, and I recalled the sound of Kevin's head knocking against the door.

"You just take it easy, pal. We don't do requests."

Max looked over at Nick and made a sweeping motion with his hand. Nick didn't do anything—he was deep in conversation with a woman who had the shoulders of a man.

Antoine had kept the beat going through this and Max and I jumped back into the song as if we'd rehearsed the whole scene beforehand. Something about the way it sounded made everyone in the lounge brighten up. Everyone cheered. Everyone but him.

When we finished *Route 66*, the man with the grenade said, "I have a grenade." He didn't yell this time, and I might have thought I'd heard him wrong if he didn't do what he did next.

He took something out of his pocket and put it on the table beside his drink. He flicked the pin of this thing with his finger, and smiled. It was a grenade, all right.

"Hey, how about playing *All of Me*?" he said.

So we played *All of Me*. The people in the lounge began to tiptoe out, leaving their coats, purses, and, in some cases, shoes behind. The man didn't pay any attention to them—even the ones who sat in front of him. He was listening to the song.

Under the circumstances I think that we played it quite well. It wasn't part of our repertoire, but we all knew the music. It might have been a little stiff, and my recollection of the lyrics was somewhat hindered by the situation: I just kept singing the same verse over and over again.

It was a difficult song to finish. How much was enough for a man like that? We might have set a record for the longest-ever version of *All of Me*, but my sense of time was probably off. He sat there watching us, wearing a sort of not-quite smile. He was so still that he looked like a photograph, or a freeze-frame in a movie. When the song tapered off and died he clapped three times.

There were only the four of us left in the room.

He stood up, pulled the pin on the grenade, and lobbed it up onto the stage. It landed inside the piano. Then he ran out the door.

The three of us hit the floor at the same time. I felt it. I closed my eyes.

Max was drinking scotch out of the bottle and lighting a fresh cigarette with the butt of an old one when they walked in.

"Here come the fuzz," he said.

Watching Max made me even dizzier than I already was. I didn't think that I could stand up for at least an hour. Two uniformed police officers had come through the door of the lounge, looking so casual that I wondered if this sort of thing happened every day.

One of the two police officers came over to the table where Max and I were sitting. The other one stayed by the door, talking to Nick and Mr. Breedle.

The officer said, "Would you two mind standing up? I understand you boys had some excitement here tonight." He had enough freckles for the three of us and unruly strands of red hair peeked out from under his hat. He was almost smiling.

"Yeah," Max said. "It was exciting all right. Better

than goddamn Disneyland. Better than Space Mountain. Thanks for coming . . . finally."

I got the impression that the man was used to people not liking him. He ignored Max and directed his questions at me.

"So what was it? A dud?"

"Not a dud, a fake. Plastic."

"May I see it?"

"It's inside the piano."

"Excuse me for a moment."

Max had been the first of us to get up. I landed under a table and might have stayed there until the cleaners came the next morning. My wrist hurt from the bad landing. My eyes were still closed when I heard Max moving around.

"Jesus fucking christ," he said.

Antoine looked shaky as he got up and I guessed that he'd had an even worse landing than me. He limped over to the piano and peered inside.

"*Mon Dieu*. What is this?"

"It's a goddamn toy is what it is. Oh daddy, I think I'm having a heart attack. Are you all right old man?"

"Yes, yes."

I don't know who called the police. Max and I sat down at a table and he started in on the scotch. We didn't say a word to each other.

The policeman came back with the grenade in a plastic baggie. He held it up to show his partner and whistled. The three of them turned to look.

"Plastic, Ed."

"Ha!"

He turned to us. "You guys should maybe think about getting day jobs."

Max smiled and his eyes twinkled. "I got a day job."

The officer took out a notepad and asked our names.

"Foster Lutz."

"Ray Brown."

"We ever met before Mr. Brown? You have a familiar face."

Max took a long pull of scotch. "I don't think so. I'm new in town. These big cities sure are exciting."

"Aren't they though?"

After the police, Nick, and Mr. Breedle left, something occurred to me. I glanced around the room. "Hey, Max. What happened to Antoine?"

Max was passing out in the chair, breathing heavily. He looked like a chubby bald baby with the bottle in his hand. His voice was weary: "Maybe he chased the guy. Maybe he went home. The fuck I know?"

"I haven't seen him since . . . since before the police got here."

Max shrugged. "I gotta take a leak."

He struggled to his feet and dropped his cigarette butt on the floor. It started to burn a mark in the carpet. Max steadied himself with the chair and shook his head.

"Grenades . . ."

The path he took to the washroom was not the shortest one. It was a sightseer's path, a wander. He waved his hands around and I could hear him cursing softly. He disappeared down the dim, stunted corridor to the side of the stage. I couldn't see him anymore but I heard him.

"Grenades!"

I was still worked up. My shoulders felt like concrete. My wrist throbbed as if it blamed me for everything. I didn't want to play anymore. I didn't want anything. And then I did. I went over to the bar to pour the first and only drink of my life.

It was gin, if I remember correctly. Whatever it was it tasted like vengeance. I took a painful sip and then drained it all away. My wrist stopped throbbing and my stomach took over. I was ready to pour another when Max emerged from the hallway.

His face was pale and mystified. He staggered up to the bar and stared at me standing there behind it under the dim light, the bottle of gin in one hand, the empty glass in the other. His eyes were all confusion.

"What're you doing?"

"My wrist hurts."

"Well . . . I think you better come to the Men's Room with me, Foster."

"What for?"

"Just come, okay?"

I followed him across the carpet and into the hallway. He was so slow in his movement that I could hardly stand it but I knew enough not to ask any more questions. When we got to the door of the Men's Room he stopped and stood there waiting.

"Go in."

I went in.

I didn't get it. It was the Men's Room. I looked at the three sinks, the four urinals, and the open window to the alley out back. The lighting was severe and the hospital-green walls were worse. There was nothing new that I could see. I stepped forward, toward the window. I looked into one of the stalls as I went, and then I saw Antoine.

His leather belt lay at his feet. His jacket was off and a sleeve pulled up. His drumsticks were sticking out of his pocket. His grin was gone.

"Antoine."

I don't know why I said that. The light in the Men's Room was glaring and I could hardly think from the noise of it. Death sitting up was the worst thing I'd ever seen in my life, and here it was again. It took my legs away and I found myself kneeling there in front of him.

Then Max was picking me up and dragging me back out into the hallway. We both sat down, facing each other, with our backs against the wall.

When I could speak I said, "Did you know he did that?"

Max didn't answer me. He stared at the floor. Maybe Antoine's spirit had possessed him at that moment. Then he looked up at me.

"I had a pretty good idea. But . . . but I figured if a guy gets to be his age he must know what he's doing."

A while later he said, "Man, he must have been the world's oldest living junky."

Chapter 6

Nadine was pulling on black stockings and black shoes. She zipped up her dress and stood looking puzzled in front of her full-length mirror. Mourning clothes did not suit her.

"I don't want to go," I said.

"Yes you do."

"I don't want to go in a taxi."

"We can't walk there, Foster. It's miles away. I'm calling one right now and you *are* coming."

I knew that I was going to go—I had to go—but for some reason I felt the need to be an infant about it. I was sitting at Nadine's kitchen table with her unread newspaper in front of me. It was morning and I'd just come over, walking through the streets with no particular urge to think or look at anything but the cracks in the sidewalk.

The newspaper was folded in half and I could only see the first three words of the headline. It was as close as I had come to current events in months.

These were the words: 'Live Aid Raises.' I wanted to know what 'Live Aid' was, and what it was raising, but I didn't pick up the newspaper. The sound of Nadine's heels clicking on the hardwood floor was paralyzing me.

The clicking stopped. "The taxi's here. Let's go."

I didn't move, and Nadine came over to the table. I was looking at her feet. She put her hand on my shoulder.

"Come on, Foster."

I looked up at her face and then I felt better. We went outside into the morning where a yellow taxi sat chugging out exhaust. We climbed in, arranged ourselves on the vinyl seats, and then the driver turned around to us. He looked like Santa Claus gone wrong.

"Where to?" he said.

Mr. Breedle paid for the coffin and the service without a word of complaint; he even did his best to track down any of Antoine's friends or relatives still living in France. People sometimes laughed at Mr. Breedle, but he was always loyal to the hotel, and would help its employees in any way he could.

He didn't find anyone. No one he spoke to had ever heard of Antoine Richelieu. The government had no records of him. He was a ghost even before he died.

None of us knew where he lived; the address and phone number in the hotel's files were long out of date. Maybe there's still a room full of his things out there somewhere, waiting for him to come home.

We decided to bury him with his sticks.

There were six of us at the funeral: Mr. Breedle, Nick, Max, Manny, Nadine, and me. The short service was held at graveside by a priest with a wide, ruddy face that looked as if it had repelled a lot of ugly weather over the years. I wondered if they let him inside, or if he just walked around the graveyard through all the days and nights of all the years, talking to God in his pipe organ voice.

We joined him in prayer, most of us mumbling along to the unfamiliar words, and then we watched as the coffin was lowered down. Beside the grave there was a small silver scoop in a bowl of loose earth. The priest motioned to it and then looked at each of us. None of us wanted to touch it.

When it was all over the priest came over to me and said, "Be well, young man."

"Okay."

Nick shook my hand and said, "Let's be friends, huh? Forget that other crap."

"Okay."

Mr. Breedle said, "Such a shame, he was a good man. With us for so many years." He put a hand on my shoulder. "Foster, why don't you take tonight off?"

"Okay."

Nadine said, "You doing all right?"

"Okay."

Max said, "Let's get the fuck out of here."

As we walked down the gravel pathway that led to the parking lot, with the arched aching limbs of the cemetery trees throwing webs of shadows across our path, Max and I fell back from the others to talk. It seemed as if there were a thousand birds screaming above us. We had to raise our voices in order to hear each other.

"Man—it just, you know, it just doesn't feel right leaving him in the ground like that. The old man doesn't belong here."

"Nobody belongs here."

"Yeah."

Max started scratching his beard and he slowed down the pace even more. "I feel like we should have stuffed him or something. So he could stay at The Underwood."

He stopped on the pathway and stood there with his mouth open. "I didn't just say that. Please don't ever remember that I said that, all right?"

How could I forget something like that? I knew what Max meant, though. It didn't feel right.

"I don't wanna get another drummer, freak."

"I don't either."

"So I guess we're a duo. Dynamic-like."

"I guess we are. But not tonight."

"No, man. Not tonight."

"We'll practice tomorrow."

"Sure we will."

I didn't want to go back to the hotel. Max drove us to Nadine's apartment in his car. He'd never mentioned that he had one. I always pictured him walking down the city sidewalks with that big bass under his arm, hordes of frightened people moving out of his way.

The car was a 1959 Plymouth-something. He took good care of it, and it still looked brand new. It was sleek, shiny black, and untouchable. I sat in the back. We drove with the windows open and I looked out at the people we passed. Max and Nadine were talking but I wasn't listening to them. Nadine shook me when we arrived and I climbed out.

Max said, "Pack a lunch. It'll be a long gone day tomorrow."

"Okay."

That week Max and I practiced for five hours a day to get our sound together. Max was spending so much time at the hotel that he sometimes had to have his customers meet him there.

Those nights that we'd played without Antoine, we had been going about it all wrong. We played like a broken trio. But in the week after Antoine's funeral we figured out that a duo was a different animal. It took us awhile to get it, but once we did we had it, we had it for good. It started to be fun again. After two weeks we moved Antoine's drum kit off the stage.

One night I was sitting at the piano, drinking a ginger ale and waiting for Max to be ready. The crowds had thinned a bit, but we figured that it had more to do with the summer weather than with us.

Max was talking on the pay phone beside the bar. Whomever he was talking to was making him angry and he kept smacking his hand against the wall. Finally he slammed down the phone and started toward me. As he walked he scanned the audience. Someone or something seemed to catch his attention because he almost tripped over an old woman's cane. He jumped up on the stage and leaned on the piano.

"Foster. You're not going to believe who's sitting over there."

"Who's sitting over there?"

"Older guy. Back table. Dig the mug on him."

He pointed at a distinguished gentleman in the far corner. The man wore a light blue summer suit, sat very still and straight, and glanced around the room as if he had been there before. He twiddled his thumbs and appeared to be in an entirely pleasant mood. The glass on his table was full of milk.

"Who is he? I've never seen him before."

"That, young man, is Lawrence Welk. I swear to you it is."

"Who's Lawrence Welk?"

"Jesus, Foster. He has a TV show. A variety show, with lots of music. Everyone in the goddamn world has seen it except you."

"Why would he be here? Are you sure it's him?"

"Positive. I saw the show yesterday. Yesterday afternoon. That's him. Crazy, man . . . Lawrence Welk at The Underwood."

Max grabbed me by the shoulders and became seriously frantic, frantically serious. "This could be our big chance. Feature this—we blow him away. He asks us to play on his show because we're so fucking good. So on we go and we're the absolute *most* and everyone in the world loves us. That's it, we're there—we're famous. We could make records, freak. Play any club, anywhere."

"TV can do that?"

"Yes. TV can do that. Do you know any polkas?"

I didn't know any polkas, but we decided to limit our repertoire to standards and sing-a-long favourites. We put a cap on our solos and tried to keep all the songs as short as possible. A middle-aged grandmother danced with her grandson. Some tone-deaf tourists belted out a few numbers with us. A fight broke out but was swiftly quelled. Some people left, and I didn't blame them. We even played *All of Me*.

We closed the set with a brief, cheery instrumental number. Lawrence Welk was still there, beaming as he sipped from a fresh glass of milk. He applauded as we climbed down from the stage. Max turned to me.

"Are you ready?"

I nodded.

"Then let's go get famous."

We strode up to Lawrence Welk's table and presented ourselves like dignitaries: hands clasped behind our backs, shoulders straight, expressions politely bemused.

"Good evening to you sir," Max said. "Did you enjoy the show?"

He was surprised that we were talking to him. He picked up his glass of milk and then put it down again. He removed a pair of glasses from his pocket and put them on. Then he peered at us through the thickness of the lenses.

"Oh, yes, I sure did enjoy the show, young fellas. It was just super. You're very talented performers."

Max put on an ill-fitting look of phony humility. "Wow. Geez. You really liked us?"

"Yes. Really."

"Because I think we'd fit in with what you've got going on—or like, *mesh*, you dig? With the theme of your show. We can play polkas, too. We can play anything. This jazz thing you saw tonight is only one facet of what young Mr. Lutz and I do. We're both really big fans of your show and your music, aren't we Mr. Lutz?"

"Huge, enormous," I said.

Lawrence Welk was shaking his head. It was easy to see that he was confused by this conversation, and that he wished it would end soon.

"Massive, gargantuan," I said.

"My show? What are you fellas talking about?"

Max took a step back. "You're Lawrence Welk."

The man laughed. It was a nervous laugh. "No, ha, I'm not Lawrence Welk, but it's not the first time that I—"

Max slapped the man on the shoulder and he almost fell out of his chair. Max had hands like pot roasts. He pointed at the man who may still have been Lawrence Welk with one of his meaty pot roast fingers, then jabbed him in the chest with it.

"Don't fuck with me. I know you're Lawrence Welk."

"Really, I swear I'm not." He motioned to Nick for his bill.

We were immobile: twin towers of idiocy. I wanted to go somewhere else and I wanted to do it fast, but Max had to make things worse.

"I guess you wouldn't happen to, like, *know* him or anything . . ."

"No. But I do know that his show went off the air in 1982." He smirked at us and put down five dollars for the milk. "I'm a big fan, too."

Later, Max explained reruns to me.

Nadine's birthday came along and I decided to take her out for dinner. She was overjoyed because we were eating somewhere other than The Underwood. I was overjoyed because the restaurant I had picked out had white napkins.

The meal came in seven courses. The pony-tailed busboy kept sneaking little looks at Nadine as he cleared but she didn't notice. We lingered over each course and finished every plate; neither of us had eaten all day.

Later, we walked home through a maze of downtown streets. The night sky over our heads was smudged starless by clouds, and off in the distance I could see spotlights spinning aimlessly across them from some invisible source. It was late in the summer and cooling down. The breeze tugged at the light fabric of Nadine's dress. I put my arm around her and we kept on walking for awhile.

The question I wanted to ask her was burning a hole in my tongue, but I needed to invent a segue. It was not something to be blurted out; I had to plan an arrival by a slow, smooth road.

This was what I said: "Hey, look at those crazy spotlights over there."

"Oh yeah."

"I wonder what they're for."

"Maybe it's a party or something."

"You want to get married?"

Now was that a segue or what?

There came a time when I felt nothing as I got up on stage to play. There was no feeling of anticipation, no joy, no gluts of nervous energy giving me goosebumps. It was a job, nothing more. Max knew what I was talking about, and together we decided to do something about it.

"We need to pull up stakes. We need to get out of this one-horse town."

"What?"

"I'll see if I can get us booked somewhere else. We'll take it from there."

I went up to the office to see Mr. Breedle, sat there in his cigarette haze, and told him that we were leaving. I think that he was expecting me to ask for a raise because he offered me one to get me to stay. He even offered to start paying Max, although he never did care for him personally. He was truly disappointed to see us go.

"What are we going to do now?" he said.

It wasn't about the money. I wasn't sure what was driving me away from there but I knew that I had to go. We got booked at a place called The Tropics three nights a week for a month, with the possibility of more if we did well there.

Max and I sat in the shiny black and chrome office of the club manager. He looked at us through a bottle of sparkling mineral water. His suntan was deep and vaguely orange.

"If the clients are hip to your thing then maybe we'll keep you on," he said.

"They'll be hip to our thing. We got the hippest thing in town."

"We'll see." He looked at me. "Mr. Lutz. Have

you ever thought about changing your name?"

The Tropics was nothing like The Underwood. It had palm trees, red stage lights, and a staff who all seemed to have been born from the same slim, blond, and smiling parents. Limousines parked in front of it and from the outside it looked like a lawyer's office.

After the last show at The Underwood I was going to move into Nadine's apartment. We never talked about it—never actually decided that it was going to happen. When I told her that we weren't going to play there anymore she told me that she'd get another key made.

"And steal a towel," she said.

The day came. The last day. I spent most of it sitting in the lounge and wondering if I was doing the right thing. Mr. Breedle had already hired my replacement. He played a synthesizer and since I didn't understand his taste in music I assumed that it was more modern than mine. I'd heard his audition. It sounded like clockwork.

I was still sitting there when I noticed that I was no longer alone. A man was standing over my left shoulder and looking at me. I turned around, "Yes?"

He was wearing sunglasses in the dimness of the lounge, a plain grey suit and a thick black tie. His face was soft and white and his hair parted with such precision that I was immediately wary of him.

"Foster Lutz."

"Yes."

"My name is Detective Dunlop."

He produced identification proving that he was indeed Detective Dunlop. When I gave it back to him he said, "I'm going to ask you some questions."

"Is this about the grenade?"

"Grenade? No. No it isn't."

There was a manila folder in his hand. He pulled some large black and white pictures out of it and began to flip through them. He took his time doing this, as if he had never seen them before.

"I'd like you to take a look at these, and then we'll talk awhile."

So, I looked at them. The pictures were of Max and a man in a pink polo shirt with blond wind-blown hair. They were standing close to a tennis court. They did various things in various shots: passing things to each other, talking, and examining their surroundings. The pictures made me feel like I was going to be sick.

"So. How do you know the man in those pictures?"

"Which man are you talking about?"

Detective Dunlop smiled at me as if I was three years old and wearing urine-soaked trousers. He removed another picture from the envelope which showed Max and I coming out of The Tropics together. Something about the way the picture was taken made us both look menacing.

"Should I ask you again?"

"We play here together. I'm a pianist."

"You're a what?"

"A piano player. He plays the bass."

"Right. And you have no idea what he does for a living?"

"No, I—"

"Come on. Don't fuck around—it won't get you anywhere. You're in serious trouble. Your friend is a drug dealer and he's going to jail. Any minute now. You're probably going to jail too, if my idea about you is right, and my ideas usually are."

"What's your idea about me?"

"My idea is that you help him sell that shit of his. It might not have seemed like you were doing much, but even knowing a guy like him could land you in jail. But . . . if you tell us what you know about him then you won't have any problems."

He paused and smiled. "See what I'm saying? Do you see how what you do doesn't affect what happens to him, just what happens to you?"

"I don't know anything about him. I don't even know where he lives."

"Well, his address is going to be changing. I hope you two didn't have any plans."

Detective Dunlop stood up and placed his card on the table. He shook his head then turned to leave.

"We're watching," he said.

I found out later how Max got caught. When Kika went back to Max her pervert cop went crazy. Perverts are passionate people. He wasn't through with Kika and couldn't resign himself to the fact that she was through with him. He wanted revenge. He waited for Kika to get off work one night and then he followed her to Max's house.

After that he began to follow Max and before long he came up with the perfect plan to get Kika back: he called his friends in the Narcotics Squad. They were interested in what he had to tell them. One of Max's tennis-playing lawyers was not what he seemed.

He was the man in the pink polo shirt with the blond windblown hair. He knew nothing of Kika.

Nadine and I got married in a small civil cere-
mony in the first week of September. It was so
small that there were only the five of us: Nadine,
me, two paid witnesses, and the man who made it
legal. It was quiet in the room, beige and empty.
Nadine and I held hands, said what we were supposed to say, and then we signed some forms and
documents. The man who made it legal kept saying,
"That's right. That's it." I think he was due for his
lunch break.

At the same time, in a building down the street,
Max's trial was just beginning. We couldn't get in
after we tied the knot because it had already started.
I heard about it later.

Max had a good lawyer. His lawyer was also a
customer, so in a way he had his own interests to
consider as well as those of his client. It was over in
less than an hour. The judge told Max that he would
be spending three months in jail.

This seemed like a lot but Max told me—the one
time that I visited him—that he got off even easier
than he'd hoped. I guess he sold a lot of grass, but I
still wouldn't know what a lot of grass was if I was
standing in it.

The one time I visited Max he said, "So when are
you two off?"

Nadine and I were going to California for our

honeymoon. I was going to get to see Route 66—the pieces of it that still existed, anyway. We were leaving the next morning in Max's 1959 Plymouth, which was his wedding present to us.

"Did you talk to my lawyer?"

"Yes."

"What did he say?"

"He said not to worry about the police. They were just trying to scare me."

"Good. You know, man, if something comes up you should stay down there. I'll be three months in here and then I don't know what, you know?"

"I'm not sure that I do. What do you mean?"

"I mean maybe you should fly solo. See what you can get hopping down there. I was only holding you back. And look at me now . . ."

He was referring to the orange jumpsuit he was wearing in the claustrophobic fluorescence of the visiting room. We were sitting at one of six tables. The room had white walls with small, barred windows on one side. There were other prisoners talking to friends and relatives and there was a trio of bored guards with pistols. Max told me that his prison was minimum security, and that most of the prisoners were in there for stealing things that didn't actually exist.

"Feature this—you should take your show to the big time."

We talked for a while longer and then our time was up. When we parted I tried to shake Max's hand but he put me in a headlock instead. One of the guards stepped forward.

"Cut that out, Brunt," he said. "How many times do I have to tell you not to fuck around?"

I went back to Nadine's and sat on the bed looking at her paintings. It was late in the afternoon and she was just home from work. She could tell that I didn't want to talk and started taking things out of her drawers for the trip.

I missed Max already and didn't see much point in playing without him. I wouldn't have known where to begin. The Tropics had cancelled our booking when they heard that it had become a solo act. But instead of depressing myself I decided not to think about it until we got back, and then I got excited thinking about our honeymoon.

Nadine said, "You better start packing. I want to leave before rush hour."

"Rush hour?"

"Just pack."

I went over to my suitcase and put everything I had into it. It took exactly one minute. I closed the lid.

"Okay, I'm done packing."

The phone rang.

Nadine picked it up. "Hello? Yes, one moment please." She held the phone toward me. "It's for you."

"It's for me?"

"Yes."

"Who is it?"

"It's a woman."

I took the phone from her and said, "Hello, this is Foster Lutz speaking, who is this please?" It had been a while since I'd used a telephone.

"Is this really Foster Lutz?"

"Yes, it is."

"My God, finally. I got this number from the hotel. I was trying to reach you there for ages. I must have called you thirty times! You didn't get my messages?"

"No."

"So. You're Foster!"

I couldn't imagine what this strange woman wanted from me. She was taking her time in getting to the point, whatever it was.

"I'm Mary West."

"Hello Mary West."

Nadine dropped the sock she was holding. She stared at me with her mouth open. "Oh my god. That's Mary West?"

"I have a TV show, Foster, have you ever heard of it?"

"I don't watch TV."

"Well, good for you. My show is very casual. I like to have a lot of variety—interviews, comedians, cooking tips, and musical performers like you. I saw you play at The Underwood Hotel some time ago. Usually I get my assistant to make these calls but I liked you so much that I wanted to talk to you myself. I've been wanting to have you as my guest on the show."

"You have?"

"Now, if you want to do this I'll send you up a plane ticket. You'll be put up in a hotel down here in L.A., and then, of course, you'll be paid for appearing on the show. Do you think you could make it down some time next week? Should I talk to your agent? I couldn't get his name."

"Don't worry about the plane tickets. I'll be there next Tuesday."

CHAPTER 7

I SAT IN THE GREEN ROOM, WHICH WAS NOT GREEN, and ate finger sandwiches not made of fingers. There was a young man sitting across from me on a brown leather sofa. The hard lustre of his clothes made mine all the more shabby, and I began to worry that I'd be mistaken for a vagrant and hauled out of the building. He was preening himself and seemed to be expecting me to say something. When I didn't he said, "So, who are you? What's your story?"

I didn't know the answer to that one yet, so I said, "I'm Foster. I play the piano."

"I'm Nathan Burton-Steele, the actor."

I nodded, and Nathan Burton-Steele kept looking at me. After a while a woman wearing a headset came in for him. He clapped his hands together and went out after her, already beaming like a throne-hungry prince.

The drive down to California took us a week. Every time that I thought we could stay on Route 66 we'd end up on an Interstate again, dodging bulky transport trucks and dough-faced lunatics in Winnebagos. Of course, Nadine did all the driving. I still wasn't a big fan of cars.

We had to get used to each other in these new surroundings, which wasn't easy at first; Nadine's clothes were always smiling but the face above them was not. We had a flat tire late one night on a deserted road, we spent a night in a motel that reeked of fumigation, and I got food poisoning from a tuna sandwich in a roadside diner. It was my first lesson in the rules of the highway.

By the time we got to California I thought that Nadine and I could handle anything, except for The Mary West Show, which I had to handle on my own. Nadine stayed in the hotel that day, still wiped out from the trip. The hotel gleamed with sterility and buzzed with friendliness. It was a monolith. People sat around the piano in the lounge and the piano player played whatever they wanted to hear, sometimes twice.

The woman with the headset came back into the Green Room. I was eating another finger sandwich and trying not to drop the filling on my suit.

"You're up Mr. Lutz."

Mary West was a young woman who'd made her name early as an actress on a children's program. Her show was new but it was already popular because she laughed all the time. After I played she had me sit down on her sofa next to Nathan Burton-Steele. The TV lights blazed and I couldn't stop blinking.

She asked me a few questions and although I wasn't trying to be funny she laughed at everything I said. The studio audience laughed right along with her—even I started laughing after awhile. The only one in the whole room who didn't laugh was Nathan Burton-Steele.

I was a hit with the disciples of daytime television. The station received a glut of calls from people asking to know more about the nice young piano player in the bad suit. Two days after I appeared on The Mary West Show I had an agent. I recorded an album—mostly standards but also a couple of my own—that same month and it sold well, for what it was. Max was right: TV could do amazing things. It amazes me more every day.

I liked it all right in California but I could tell that Nadine felt out of place. I was more out of place than her, but because I was out of place everywhere it didn't bother me so much.

All the parties we went to felt like work. I met

hundreds of people and they all gave me business cards. My pockets bulged with business cards and money. After one of those parties Nadine said, "I can't stand it here anymore. It's phony."

"Mr. Harriman thinks I should do a tour. Let's do it, you and me."

A nd so we did. We took that black untouchable car back out on the highway and we went anywhere that would have us. We were nomads—the king and queen of the road. There was no stopping us.

The clubs in which I played were small, but we didn't need much money to get around. Nadine took care of the itinerary and publicity; she talked to club managers and radio people and she found us places to stay. She was talking all the time, and she was good at it. But the two of us weren't talking much anymore. We were swimming in details.

As we drove through the prairies one endless winter day I was staring out the window trying to determine where the expanse of dirty snow met the expanse of dirty sky. I couldn't, and it was making me crazy. We passed a road sign, and then I turned to her.

"Two hundred and seventy-nine miles to go," I said.

"Your turn to drive soon."

"What time do you think we'll get there?"

"Between 6:00 and 7:00."

"And I'm on at 8:00, right?"

"Yes, you're on at 8:00."

I turned back to the window.

I said goodbye and hung up the telephone. A monstrous artificial palm stood brooding in the truck stop foyer like a bored sentry. Walking toward our table I passed the kitchen door and was hit by a stench of grease and cigar smoke. A sign dangled over the long orange countertop, glowing sickly under the flickering lights, announcing the Breakfast Special.

Nadine was sitting at a booth by the front window, just the back of her head visible over the top of the seat. The only other occupied table held two elderly women chasing nibbles of toast with sips from their coffee cups. They smiled and nodded at me. I took my place across from Nadine.

"What'd Mr. Harriman have to say?"

"He might have found me a job writing the music for a movie."

"What's it about?"

"I think it's about police chasing drug dealers. He said they can't pay me a whole lot of money but I could do other things while I was there."

The waitress shuffled up to us with a tray of coffee and ice water, her hair in a high-tensile bun that pulled her face into a taut semblance of a smile. She set down the cups and glasses and then removed a pad and pencil from her apron.

"Yes?"

Nadine ordered banana pancakes. I asked for brown toast, and eggs sunny-side up. I've always remembered that.

The waitress shook her head. "The cook doesn't stand for any fanciness. How about scrambled?"

I didn't care because of the way that Nadine was looking at me. I realized then that she hadn't looked at me for weeks, not like this. She reached over to the window and raised the venetian blind some. Then she started playing with the ice in her water glass.

"Foster. I'm going home for awhile."

"Home?"

"Wooster. The farm."

"When?"

"Tomorrow."

Nadine and I made an agreement. We said goodbye at the train station and I told her that after
I'd done the things I had to do in California I'd go up
to see her.

But the horizon of things that I had to do kept
expanding. After I finished the music for the movie,
Mr. Harriman told me that I should record another
album. And then after that there would be publicity
and another tour. I called Nadine.

"What do you think I should do?"

"I think Mr. Harriman's right. I think you should
do what he says."

This was not the answer that I wanted to hear.

We spoke once or twice after that, but our con-
versations were so stilted and shallow that I
stopped calling her. She didn't call me either, but a
lawyer did, a year later. We divorced through the
mail. I imagined lines of suitors already stretching
up and down those country roads. Sometimes I
hated my imagination.

Once I was driving north and got lost in miles
and miles of farmland. I stopped when I saw something familiar. What I saw was a big brown grain
elevator. As it turned out, I was passing through

Wooster. I got out of the car and looked at the farm-house brooding there down a weedy dirt driveway.

There was smoke coming out of the chimney and I thought I saw people moving around inside. I got back into the car and drove away, looking at the grain elevator in the rearview mirror. It was enormous.

Sometime after that I was back in California, flipping through the Count Basie section in a gleaming, three-leveled record store. The music they were playing was thunderous and the lyrics incomprehensible but it had a lot of energy and everyone else seemed to enjoy it. People were moving everywhere, brushing past and bumping into me. One of these people said my name.

"Hello, Foster!"

"Well, hello, Mary West."

"How are you?"

"I'm okay, I'm fine."

"What are you doing right now? Do you have time for lunch?"

"Sure."

We took a table in an Italian restaurant down the street. We stayed there for hours. Mary West still laughed all the time and had the ability to make everyone around her laugh as well. People at other tables were laughing and a few of them even asked for her autograph. I was happy to see her again.

As we walked back out into the mayhem of the street Mary West turned to me, smiling. "We should do this again, Foster. Soon."

"We should."

We did do it again. I was staying in California for awhile, busy making records and writing music for movies, TV shows, and commercials. We began to see each other all the time. I started spending weekends at her beach house. We took trips together, and bought each other presents. Mary West was lonely, despite the fact that everyone who watched TV seemed to love her. Eventually, I seemed to love her too.

I held the razor under the brass taps and then brought it back to my face. I slid it up my neck and the tearing sound of my whiskers was huge in the silence of the beach house. I was alone, just out of the shower, and convinced that something was wrong.

Mary West's bathroom was regularly photographed for interior design magazines. It was a miracle made up of Mexican tile and factory-aged wood; it had a bay window overlooking the ocean, three skylights, tropical plants, a massive clawfoot tub, and an antique mirror from a Spanish monastery. It was my favourite room in the house.

I ran the razor along my jawline, watching myself in the mirror but thinking of something else. When shaving you should only be thinking about shaving—I winced when I nicked off a piece of my chin. I stood there looking in the mirror and waited for the blood to run through the shaving soap. It made a line from my chin down to my collarbone. I didn't move for a long time.

When I did, I went out into the living room. I passed the deep stone fireplace, the pair of plush blue sofas, and the coffee table that once belonged to Charlie Chaplin. Over by the window sat my piano. If I was sitting at it I could look out across the ocean and wait for the sunset. It was beautiful, but not that day.

I sat down on the bench and watched the mad multitudes of seagulls squawking and fighting over scraps of dead fish. A few people lay out on the beach and two women threw a frisbee back and forth at the waterline.

I turned to the piano and started playing some-thing that I'd been working on—not for money, but for myself. I didn't like the sound of it.

I wiped the blood off of my neck and smeared it across the keys. I closed my eyes, clenched my fists, and began to play something random, tuneless, and loud. It was the first music I'd made in months.

I am in my old room in The Underwood—Room 136. I told Mary West that I was going out of town to meet with a record producer when all I was actually planning was to get away somewhere. I ended up here, and have been here for two days. It's comfortable here, and I'm afraid that I might get stuck again.

My room hasn't changed but everything else has. The lobby is in ruin. The pale yellow paint is peeling off the walls like dead skin, and the carpet is threadbare, grease-streaked, and mottled with burns. I couldn't stay in the lounge for long. It was full of lonely drunks with trays of beer, and there was a karaoke machine where my piano used to be.

No one I know is left. Mr. Breedle passed away a few years ago and the new manager must not care about legacies—or anything else. Even the pictures upstairs are gone, but I can't imagine where.

I was never able to track down Max after he got out of jail. Until yesterday, that is, when I passed his lawyer in the street. He told me that Max had used the money he'd saved up selling grass to move to another city, and had bought himself into a nightclub there. Max's lawyer told me the name of the club and I got the phone number from the operator. When he picked up it sounded as if he was in the middle of a riot. I guessed that he was the ringleader.

"Yeah?"

"Max. It's Foster."

"What? Talk louder!"

"It's Foster!"

"Foster?! Get outta here! Is that really you, freak?!"

"Yes!"

"Too much! Where are you?!"

"I'm at The Underwood! I'm in my old room!"

"Is that place still standing?"

"Barely!"

"What the hell are you doing there?!"

I couldn't lie to him.

"I don't know."

～

P.G. TARR was born in Vancouver. He currently lives in Toronto and is working on a collection of short stories. This is his first published work.